The Naked Eye

Catherine Ennis

THE NAIAD PRESS, INC.
1998

Printed in the United States of America on acid-free paper
First Edition

Editor: Lila Empson
Cover designer: Bonnie Liss (Phoenix Graphics)
Typesetter: Sandi Stancil

Library of Congress Cataloging-in-Publication Data

Ennis, Catherine, 1937 –
The naked eye / by Catherine Ennis.
p. cm.
ISBN 1-56280-210-0 (alk. paper)
1. Lesbians – Fiction I. Title.
PS3555.N6N35 1998
813'.54—dc21

98-13223
CIP

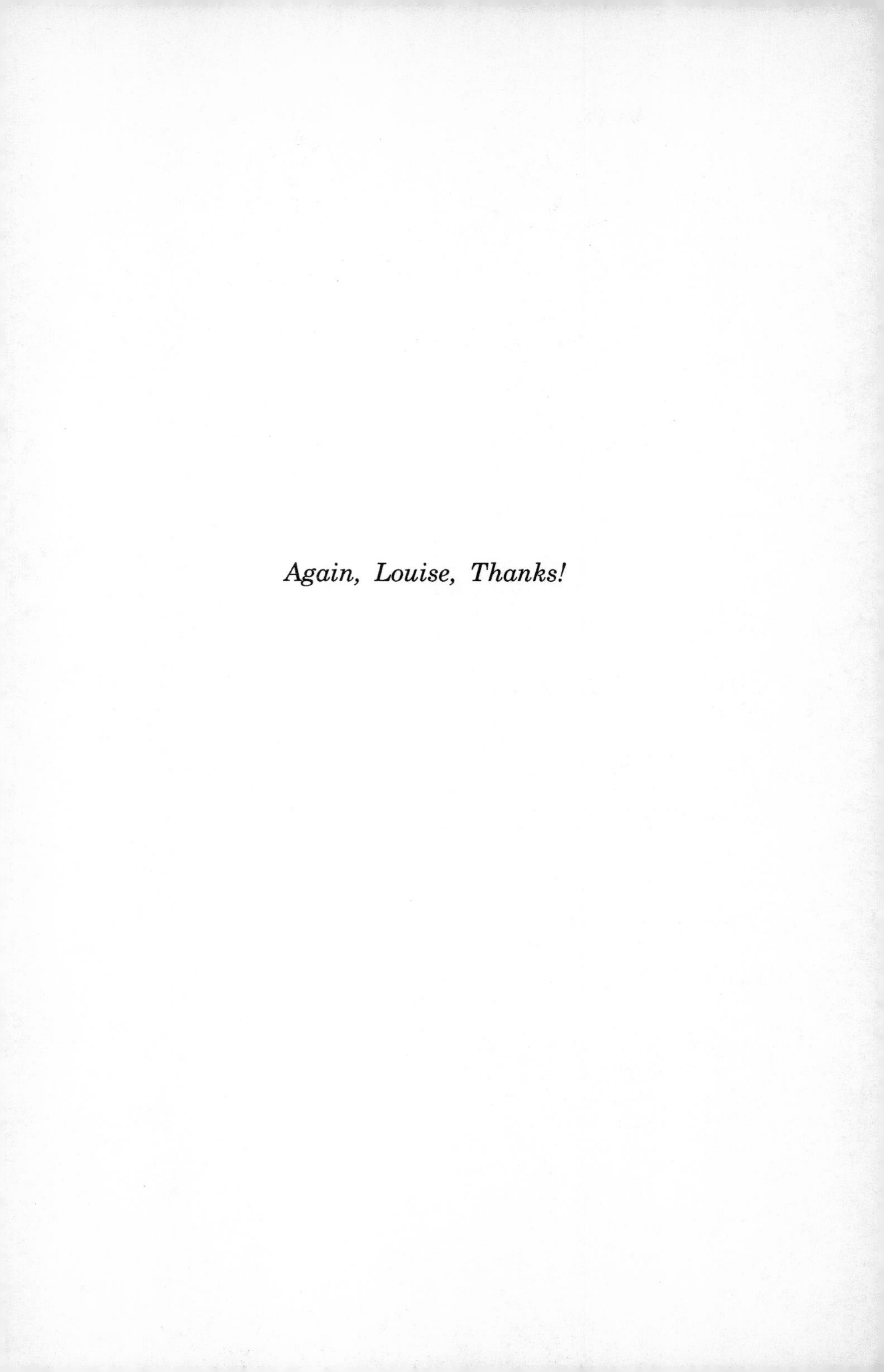

Again, Louise, Thanks!

About the Author

Catherine Ennis lives in a small but rapidly growing community north of New Orleans. Her present family consists of one lover and three cats. She works very hard at not working anymore and enjoys writing, eating, and gossiping with her many friends in the northshore area (not necessarily in that order).

This is her seventh novel.

Chapter 1

Katherine Duncan didn't know that shafts of sunlight, filtering through the trees directly overhead, centered on her like a spotlight, making her auburn hair a beacon against the green and brown foliage of the swamp.

Except for her shining hair, she was almost invisible in camouflage shirt and pants. Her battered canoe was dark green. Even the inside had been painted dull green at one time. Katherine merged into the background, becoming part of the swamp.

She held herself perfectly still; only her fingers

and eyes moved as she refocused on two heron chicks awaiting their next feeding. There was a rush of wings and, as the adult slowed for a landing, the chicks started jerking and squawking. Katherine began taking a series of shots, the soft whirring of the camera unnoticed by the busy family group. When the adult's feet lit on the jumble of loose sticks that made up their nest, both chicks reared and reached for food, yellow bills gaping. The camera caught every move.

The rookery was crowded with new heron families, but Katherine had zeroed in on this particular nest. Her canoe eased to a perfect fit between several adjacent cypress knees. An opening in the underbrush, while concealing her, gave a clear view of the nest and its occupants.

The chicks never seemed to get enough food. But after photographing them from the time they were barely out of the egg to now, when the anxious youngsters hopped greedily in her camera's eye, Katherine felt she had what she wanted. Carefully she dismantled the camera and attachments, snugging them into a large, waterproof bag. After zipping the container closed she pushed with her hands on the knee tips and backed the canoe away from the nest. The herons ignored her.

"So long, guys," Katherine said softly. Smiling, she picked up her short paddle and began maneuvering through the foliage, avoiding the debris that bobbed free in the dark water and the many cypress knees that grew in profusion near the mother trees. She noticed that most knees were partly submerged now; the water had risen a couple of inches since the day before. The whole swamp seemed to be flowing in a quiet rush toward the river. As she paddled, she saw leaves and small floating things come abreast before silently gliding past. *If the water gets much higher,* she thought, *the nests will flood.*

As she moved away from the rookery, sunlight, spotted through the green canopy, again touched her hair. Katherine's clothing and canoe blended with the shadows, but the flashes of deep auburn made it easy to follow her winding progress toward the shallow waterway entrance into the swamp.

Two dark eyes, shaded by the bill of a baseball cap, watched from the concealment of an ancient cypress clump as Katherine eased her canoe along the narrow ditch and into the river. Until Katherine turned upstream, the watcher stood, unmoving. When Katherine was out of sight, he slowly poled his pirogue back into the swamp.

A handwritten note was tacked to the cottage door. *Eat at five-thirty*, it said, *and we'll play poker after*. Katherine glanced at her watch. Time enough for a shower. She stood under a warm spray, thinking about the chicks.

There had been three eggs at first, she remembered. Only two had hatched, and she had recorded every movement as the first chick emerged, wet and ugly. The other baby pecked its way into the world sometime later. When Katherine returned the next morning, the second tiny chick was dry, hungry, and flopping about uncontrollably. "Only a mother could love you," she told them, but they hadn't cared about looks; food was all important.

Hair still damp, Katherine walked across the grassy compound to a cabin composed of two rooms and a screened porch larger than hers. No one answered her knock, so she opened the door and walked through to the kitchen. No one greeted her, but four places were set at the long wooden table, and something that smelled delicious was bubbling on the stove over a low fire.

Guests for dinner tonight, Katherine thought. Archie loved company and would have dragged strangers off the street if those she invited couldn't come. Since her cooking was the best in the parish, it would have been sheer folly for anyone to pass up a meal at her table.

Katherine fixed a glass of tea and was about to sit on the worn living room couch when the screen door opened.

"Your trailer won't get water in it even if the river rises another couple of feet," Archie was saying over her shoulder. "And it won't wash away. We go through these floods every year. There'll be a few snakes —" Archie caught sight of Katherine and stopped abruptly. The two women following almost crashed into her back.

"Here's my favorite person," Archie announced, her smile broadening. "Y'all, this is Katherine Duncan. She's here to take pictures of our swamp and the heron rookery down river . . . for a book . . . for the university."

"And these two ladies," she added, pointing, "have that trailer by the big oak tree. Betty and Nina are both schoolteachers from Texas."

Katherine smiled; Betty and Nina smiled and nodded; and Archie herded them into the kitchen.

"Sit where you like," she told them. "There's nothing formal about eating at my house."

Supper was gumbo, thick, delicious, and steaming hot. White rice, home-baked garlic bread, and iced tea topped off the meal. Betty and Nina had seconds, which pleased Archie. "I'm going to send a bowl to your trailer," she announced.

After the meal, Archie shooed them out of the kitchen, leaving cleanup chores for later. "I may even wait till tomorrow. Or," she joked, "I may let the flood do it. It depends on how fast the river rises, of course. TV said the rain has not stopped up north, so we can expect more water. They haven't figured out yet how high it'll crest or when . . . sometime in the next week, I guess."

Betty leaned forward in her chair. "You're sure we won't be in any danger?" she asked. "Shouldn't we move our trailer to higher ground just to be safe? And what about snakes?"

"Your trailer is already on high ground, honey. Couple of years ago I was neck-deep in water right here where we're sitting, but I'm in a kind of hollow that fills pretty fast. You don't have to worry about snakes. They're only looking for a place to keep dry; they won't bother you. Now, I have some homemade pear ice cream y'all are gonna like. I'll be right back."

Betty looked at Katherine. "Your book is about birds?" she asked politely.

"Yes and no. I have a contract to capture, in photographs, the seasonal changes in a Louisiana swamp. The swamp downriver from here isn't the size of the Atchafalaya, but it's very old and has a long history of Indian occupation." Katherine paused, knowing her interest and enthusiasm probably weren't shared by two vacationing teachers from Texas.

But Betty was clearly interested. Frowning slightly, she asked, "Did Indians live in the swamp?"

"Again, yes and no," Katherine answered. "They lived along the coastline, at the mouth of the rivers that flow into Lake Pontchartrain, and they hunted in the swamp: muskrat, beavers, alligators, frogs, snakes . . . whatever they considered edible. Indian artifacts turn up all around here."

"Have you ever found anything?" Nina also sat forward, her elbows on her knees. "I love to dig around," she explained; "I've never found anything, though."

"Yes, I've found pottery shards dating back to about 200 B.C."

"How can you tell?" Both women spoke at once.

"From the way the pieces were decorated. Each period had different, identifiable designs. There are several drawings of pottery designs from separate cultures that occupied this area over the years," Katherine explained. "If you want to see some pottery shards, ask Archie. She has basketfuls."

Betty thought for a moment. "Are you going to add anything about the Indians in your book?"

Katherine shook her head. "No, I was interested only in the swamp itself. I've been living here since last spring, and I thought I had shot enough until Archie told me about the rookery." Katherine smiled, remembering the day she and Archie paddled farther into the swamp than she would ever have gone alone, and her excitement as they watched the heron's nest building.

"That's when I decided to photograph the birds too," Katherine continued. "I've followed one family all the way from the first egg to pinfeathers on the babies. I wanted to photograph the juveniles until the time they were ready to leave the nest, but the flood may make that impossible."

With a slight shrug, Katherine added sadly, "I've grown fond of those babies."

"I think we'd like a copy of your book when it's ready."

"That's great, Betty. Give me your address and when it's printed I'll have one sent to you." *This is fine,* Katherine thought, *my first sale and I haven't even seen this week's film.*

By morning the water had risen another couple of inches and was lapping at Archie's garden. "You shouldn't go out today, Katherine," Archie warned. "No telling what's floating out there. The current won't be too strong yet and the water hasn't risen much, but it's deeper and moving faster so it'll pick up stuff that's been stuck on the bottom. You don't want to run into a floater that you couldn't see."

"No, but I know the way to the rookery, and I'll be careful. I'd also like to know what happens to wildlife when nature floods an area, like what's happening to the swamp now." Katherine finished her coffee. "Anyway, I need to know if my baby herons are OK."

"They're likely to get you killed, is what. If you're not back by about one or two, I'm calling the river patrol."

* * * * *

Going downriver was easy. The water wasn't very high, but it was moving faster than it had looked from Archie's boat ramp. Katherine needed her paddle only to keep the canoe midpoint in the river. With the water rushing her along, she passed the hidden waterway that led into the rookery. When she saw two power lines crossing overhead, she knew she'd gone too far. Turning the canoe back upriver was not simple. Paddling against the normal rush of the Tangipahoa's dark water required strength and skill, but with the river swollen and surging toward the lake faster than usual, Katherine needed to dig in with her paddle to make any headway at all.

A narrow, shallow waterway, hidden by low-hanging branches and thick foliage, led her inland from the river. For half a block the greenery was so dense on both sides that the branches met overhead. Katherine pushed her paddle against the muddy bottom to move the canoe forward, dodging leaves and limbs that were lower than they had been the day before.

The water's higher, that's why, Katherine thought as she pushed aside a tupelo gum branch that was aimed at her face. She gave one last shove of the paddle and floated free. There was always water enough in the swamp to float her light canoe, but now the few, scattered islands of dry land were submerged, and the water, usually mirror calm, was alive with ripples as it swirled past obstacles in its rush to get to the river.

Katherine held the canoe still with the paddle braced against a stump while she looked around. "My landmarks are gone!" she said with astonishment. Faced by a sea of moving water broken only by trees and leaves, she was totally without direction.

I don't need the islands anymore, she thought, after surveying the area. *I can orient myself with the help of the sun and head directly west.* It took twice as long because the sun's location, seen through the greenery, seemed to change. She breathed a sigh of relief when she recognized the rookery and her special nest where they were supposed to be. An adult heron was busy with feeding chores. Both babies were squawking and lurching, and they paid not one iota of attention as Katherine slowly floated her canoe to its usual stop.

The babies were OK, judging by their appetite, and were not concerned that water was lapping at the low branch that held their nest. The nest would be submerged if the water rose another six inches.

Unpacking her camera, she took a few shots of the babies and of the adult bird, mother or father; then she moved the canoe to a clearing and, carefully standing, took a panoramic view of the swamp and the rushing water. Another series focused on the foreground foliage, leaving the far swamp unclear, as if a light fog had rolled in. For a moment she thought she saw movement in the distance but, after peering carefully and seeing nothing, decided she was mistaken.

Later, as Katherine searched for the tiny concealed ditch that cut through the riverbank and allowed her access to the river, she kept thinking about the nest and the babies. *They'll be gone*, she acknowledged, *swept away when the water crests, and I probably can't get back in here when the water is much higher, even if I want to.* Discouraged, she tried to stop thinking about the babies' fate.

Once in the river, Katherine had to paddle furiously to make headway upstream. Archie was waiting on the dock, hands on her hips. "Girl, I was going in to call the patrol," she said as she helped Katherine take her gear out of the canoe. "I hope you know this was your last trip downstream."

Together they carried the canoe to higher ground near the oak tree. "Y'all come have a beer," Betty called from her trailer door.

"Katherine can," Archie yelled back. "I'd better start moving my outdoor stuff. Water's coming up fast now."

"Thanks, Betty." Katherine waved. "Think I'd better help Archie with the moving."

As they walked across the sandy yard, Archie took Katherine's arm. "Honey, I heard a little while ago that the river won't be cresting as high as first supposed, so we're gonna be OK after all. I might get a few drops in my house, but that's nothing new. I told Betty and Nina, and they seemed real happy about it. I'm gonna take them to the mouth of the river when the water goes down some so they can look for pieces of pottery. Wouldn't they be excited if they found an arrowhead?"

Katherine nodded. "That will be great, Archie."

When they neared Archie's cabin, Katherine said, "If I can't get back to the rookery, Archie, I'm finished here. I still have a couple of weeks or so at the studio in New Orleans. They're going to do some more enlarging and color stuff for me before I begin selecting the prints I want for the book. Then we have to edit text, but I can do that in New Orleans, too." Katherine thought for a moment, "I'll start getting my things together, and then in the morning I'll head back to the Big Easy."

"Honey, you're welcome to stay here forever. You know that, don't you?"

"I wish I could, my friend, I really wish I could."

"Well, eat with me tonight. I have some fresh gator tail, and I know you've never tasted it. I'm cooking it in a red sauce that'll blow you away. What say?"

"I'll try anything once. Five-thirty OK?"

Chapter 2

Alligator meat was OK, Katherine decided. At first the idea of eating alligator was daunting, but with Archie's magic spoon in the cooking pot, the meal became an experience worth repeating.

"I had no idea," Katherine said, folding her napkin. "This was delicious." At Archie's pleased smile, Katherine added, "I've never seen alligator in a meat counter, so where did you get it?"

"My friend Danny poaches for a living. He lives downriver on the shell ridge, and he brings me little treats. I let him use my phone occasionally so that he doesn't have to go up to the highway. He doesn't have a car, you know."

Katherine blinked. "A poacher?" she asked. This should not have been a surprise. Archie knew everyone in this area of the parish; why wouldn't she know a poacher if he lived nearby?

"Sure," Archie said. "The swamp hides more than a handful of regulars. They make a living on skins. They trap and fish . . . whatever sells."

"Sounds like you know these people."

"Honey, how do you think I got this property?" Archie reached for Katherine's plate, stacking it on top of her own. She leaned closer, gave Katherine a broad wink, and said, "River frontage is worth gold these days, and I own a half mile or thereabouts. All thanks to a husband who sold what the hunters brought in, then bought land along the river, including this place. Honey, we made a bundle forty years ago." Archie's smile broadened. "They were hunters then. Now they're poachers."

Katherine had thought Archie supported herself from the rental of one rather shabby cabin and two trailer lots perched on a sandy rise at one of the river's deep bends. "I don't think I've seen anybody in the swamp, poacher or not. Where were they when I was there?"

"Well, they saw you. They knew where you were every minute. Did you think I'd let you wander alone in that place? You'd never have found your way out. Why, the gators would have made a meal of you the first day. No, my friends knew you were there. They kept an eye out."

"Today was the first time I've seen anybody. At least I saw something moving that wasn't a bird or a deer." Katherine remembered the feeling that there was a body other than her own on the far edge of the rookery.

"Probably Danny." Archie pushed back her chair and, ignoring the stacked plates, said, "Let's have coffee."

As Katherine walked to her cabin, she looked toward the trailer under the oak. No lights. *Probably in bed early*, she thought, smiling. I'll bet they're gay, and I'll bet I know what they're doing right now. She sighed, picturing long-ago vacation nights in a VW camper with Pam. Even now she could feel her head banging their small ice-box as Pam nuzzled and thrust. The memory of Pam's busy fingers made Katherine aware of a creeping dampness between her legs.

Either celibacy has made me horny as hell or alligator tail is an aphrodisiac, she thought. *A cold shower should fix that.*

The shower wasn't cold. Katherine washed her hair, standing for long minutes under a warm stream, her thoughts now turned to the two heron chicks. She wondered if they had already been washed away, parents helpless as the rushing water sucked the tiny bodies under.

Katherine, wrapped in a towel, remembered that the hair dryer was stored away in her duffel bag. She reached for the overhead light switch as she started out of the bathroom.

"Don't turn that on!" A woman's voice, deep and authoritative came from the darkened room in front of her.

Katherine's breath caught in surprise. She faced the shadowy figure. "What are you doing here? I thought you were still in Mobile."

"Just passing through, so I stopped to see you, of course. Thought I'd give you another chance."

Katherine stiffened, her hand reaching to secure the towel. "I don't want a chance. Get the hell out of here, Pam." She could feel her voice trembling. "I told you I didn't ever want to see your face again."

"Naw, babe, you didn't mean that." Pam yanked the edge of the towel, pulling it from Katherine's grasp. "I like it when you're naked," she said gruffly, moving so that they were almost touching. "I like to feel you like this . . ." Her arms encircled Katherine's waist, pulling Katherine into a rough embrace. Her lips nibbled across Katherine's cheek. "I came all this way just to spend the night with you."

"Stop, damn it!" Katherine turned her face away, pushing against Pam's shoulders. "Let me go!" Struggling, her elbow managed to land one solid smack against Pam's left ear. Instantly Katherine knew her mistake. Flinching, she held her arms against her chest and ducked her head in protection against the blow that was more sensed than seen.

"Aw, honey, I'm not going to hit you anymore. Didn't I promise?" Pam's arms were gentle as she pulled Katherine against her. One hand cupped Katherine's breast; the other guided Katherine's head so that their lips met. “I’m gonna give you a whole night of lovin’. Like you always wanted.”

Knowing struggle was useless, Katherine forced her body to relax. She felt Pam’s hand moving against her flesh, Pam’s tongue wet, probing. “Please don’t,” she whispered, turning her head away. “Please.”

“Please more?” Pam leaned to Katherine’s breast, her warm mouth circling a nipple. “I’ll give you more, baby, all you want.” In an instant, Pam’s fingers were searching through Katherine’s pubic hair, causing Katherine to stiffen as exploration stopped and fingertips touched wetness.

Katherine’s impulse was to spread her legs, to lie naked on the cabin floor and give her body to Pam. She heard Pam’s hoarse breathing, felt her own heart thudding, and knew her need, her desperate need, for Pam to continue.

Twisting, she broke from Pam’s embrace. “Keep your hands off me, you bastard.” The towel was bunched around her feet. She snatched it and, with trembling hands, wrapped it around her body again.

“It’s not over between us, babe. You’re hot for me right now, aren’t you?” Pam moved a step, her grin widening as Katherine backed away. “We were good together, remember?” She held out her arms.

“Get out,” Katherine hissed.

“I don’t know what you’re so pissed about. You’ve had a year to get over your mad. What is it? You want more time?”

“I want you out of here.” Katherine stepped to the door and grasped the knob. “You betrayed me with everybody on two legs. Why should I want you back?" It was a mistake to open any kind of dialogue, Katherine realized. Pam would never understand.

"Aw, they didn't mean anything. You always did make mountains out of molehills. I told you I was sorry, didn't I?" Her expression was one of innocent disbelief.

Katherine opened the door. "Out!" she said. "There's nothing between us anymore."

"You're probably fucking somebody else, that's what. Well, I'll give you time for that to wear off, and then I'll be back." Shoving Katherine aside, Pam stomped through the door. Katherine watched as she crossed the grassy compound, heading for the parking lot.

Another shower did little to calm Katherine. *What do I really feel?* she asked herself. *Anger or shame?* That fleeting moment when she wanted Pam's lovemaking was, even in memory, still strong enough to create an ache between her legs.

The water heater had run out of hot water, but Katherine didn't mind. She scrubbed and rinsed, moving slowly, welcoming the coolness. *Why did I let it go on for so long?* she questioned again. *Pam betrayed me and beat me black-and-blue more times than I can remember. What kept me with her?* Katherine knew the answer well. It had to do with passion and desire and orgasmic pleasures.

Katherine dried herself, flipped out the light, and lay naked on the bed. Sleep wouldn't come. Memories were too clear. With the outside light bright in her window, Katherine stared at the ceiling, her tears streaming.

"Someone fishtailed out of here last night and left tire tracks a foot deep in the sand." Archie was clearing the table. "It could have been those boys raggin' me again."

Katherine was sipping coffee, both elbows on Archie's kitchen table, the cup balanced between her hands. "No, I had a guest," she said, "a woman I used to live with a year ago. We argued and she left mad."

"From the holes she dug, I'm surprised she didn't get stuck." Archie had noticed the puffiness around Katherine's eyes. "Are you OK, hon? You don't seem your usual cheerful self, but I thought it was because you were leaving today."

"I'm fine," Katherine said with a tiny smile. "I"m going to miss you, though. We've had some good times."

Archie sat. "You know I'll have room for you if you need to take some more pictures."

"Yes, I know that," Katherine smiled. "Do me a favor?"

"You want to know what happens to the chicks, don't you?"

Katherine nodded. "You know which nest. Could you check on them as soon as the water goes down? Without risking life and limb, of course."

“Sure I will. And I’ll call you at that temporary number in New Orleans.” Archie clearly doubted there would be chicks or nest, but she kindheartedly said she would take a look anyway.

“I may not be at that number. I’ve decided to stay in New Orleans, get an apartment, maybe open a studio. If I do that, my phone number will change. I’m going to keep in touch, though.”

“Honey, you’d sure better do that. You’re family now, you know.”

Katherine reached across the table, taking Archie’s hand in her own. “I know, darling,” she said softly. “I feel that way, too.”

Archie stood, took a pencil from the glass jar next to the phone, and scribbled something on a scrap of paper. Handing the paper to Katherine, she said, “Call this number when you get to town. This is my niece. She sells houses, and she’ll find an apartment for you right off. I’ll tell her you’re coming.”

Rushing water undercut a tall willow. In falling, the willow broke through a dam of jumbled sticks, releasing plastic sacks that had floated to a stop against them. Obstruction gone, bumping and jostling in the current, the sacks began moving toward the river.

Some were dragged along the bottom, halting when they were snagged. Then, as the current tore them loose, they began the journey again.

Floaters, those sacks that enclosed air and were tightly sealed, began sailing grandly over what would have halted them before the flood. Many were pierced, and intruding water caused them to sink. These joined others on the bottom, some tearing apart enough to release their cargo, but dragged or floating, their destination was the river, and eventually Lake Pontchartrain.

The herons saw. Small animals and snakes taking refuge on tree limbs saw. Alligators, unhappy about the rushing water, saw. Human eyes saw, but they knew the sacks for what they were.

Katherine took the causeway to New Orleans. Twenty-four miles of flat, gray water and the thump, thump of tires on the concrete spans numbed her mind. She could not seem to turn her thoughts from Pam and their encounter last night.

Pam had been Katherine's second lesbian relationship. Her first had been a one-night stand with a married neighbor. *I am not going to get involved with anyone until I've known them for ten years*, Katherine thought, *then maybe I'll hop into bed. Why have I had such terrible luck?*

At the end of the causeway, Katherine slowed to turn into a gas station with an outside phone. She dialed, and a pleasant female voice answered. When Katherine identified herself, the voice said, "I have a place for you to look at. Archie told me what you might like. If you have time, we can meet right now."

Katherine drove down Esplanade Avenue, slowing when the house numbers began to get close to the number Archie's niece had given her. She shook her head when she saw a house number that matched.

The identifying numerals were on a tall, iron fence, fronting what could only be called a mansion with huge white columns and wide steps leading up to the tallest, widest glass doors Katherine had ever seen. "There is no way I can rent this," Katherine said under her breath. "The damn fence probably cost a half million, and that was at least a hundred years ago."

She had to push with both hands to move the heavy gate. At least twenty steps led up to the veranda where a short, dark-haired woman was seated in a wicker rocker.

"Hi," she said, "I'm Kay, and you must be Katherine. I just had to come up here and sit. This wicker furniture is the real thing, try it." She pointed to the next chair. "Wouldn't you just give an arm and leg?"

Katherine didn't particularity care about wicker, one way or the other, but the rocker fit like it had been molded to her body. "It's comfortable," she agreed with a slight shrug, "but I can't afford this house. What I wanted was an apartment, something with reasonable rent." She looked inside at the twelve-foot ceiling. "This place is way too big for me."

"Oh, it's not the house. There's an apartment on the third floor, a converted attic, that's positively gorgeous. I have strict orders about who gets to see it, and you fit like a glove. The woman who owns it lives on the first two floors, and she thinks it's a waste to have the apartment empty."

Chapter 3

It was gorgeous. The carpet was deep, a pleasant dark contrast to the light green of the walls, and all the woodwork was a soft, creamy white. After Katherine walked through the kitchen, and the spacious bedroom with king-size bed and dormer windows facing City Park, she turned to Kay, awed. "I wouldn't have believed an attic could look like this."

Kay laughed, "Wait till you see the closets. They're to die for."

"Closets, too?"

"Big enough to park your car, honey. There's even a tiny office next to the bedroom."

Katherine looked around. "Has anyone ever lived here? It looks brand-new."

"Miss Weathers, the lady who owns the house, lived up here, but she's moved downstairs." Kay led Katherine to a large door in the living room wall. "We came up the outside stairs, but this leads down to the main floor and the front doors you saw from the veranda."

"So you could enter or leave from the outside stairs or walk through the house?"

"Yep, like if it was raining." Kay thought for a moment, her forehead wrinkled as she recalled the rental description. "It's completely furnished, even linens and kitchen stuff. There's no washer or dryer, but there's a place in the next block. Also, Miss Weathers didn't insist on a damage deposit, and utilities are included in the rent."

"That's odd."

"Not really. Miss Weathers explained that the apartment was built as an extension of the main house, so there wasn't any reason to have separate utilities."

"Well," Katherine said, "I think it's perfect, even with stairs to climb. It's probably way out of my reach, though."

Kay named a figure, her eyes twinkling.

"You're kidding!"

"Nope, you hand me a check and the place is yours. Move in this afternoon, if you like."

"What about the landlady? When will I meet her?" Katherine opened her checkbook.

"Well, she comes and goes. You may not see her for weeks. She owns three flower shops in town, but she doesn't always stay here. You'll like her, though."

Busy writing, Katherine looked up. "I have a car. What about parking?"

"That's the one drawback as I see it. You'll have to park on the street, I'm afraid. There is a driveway but Marlena uses it."

"Marlena is my landlady?"

"Marlena Weathers, yes. This house has been in her family since before the war. And, except for the short time when Yankees billeted a group of officers here, it's been occupied by Marlena's family. Lots of history to this place, you know."

Katherine put the check in Kay's outstretched hand. "Now that it's mine, I think I'll look at the rest of it. I suppose there's a bathroom?"

Several hours later, Katherine dropped, exhausted, into the soft comfort of the living room couch. She had moved her clothes and cameras upstairs, found a neighborhood grocery for coffee and the few food items she might need while she settled in, and made the huge bed with clean-smelling linens from a closet jammed with bath-and-bed accessories. And it wasn't even dark yet.

This is too perfect, Katherine thought. *I just hope Miss Weathers doesn't turn out to be some dried-out, nosy prune. I haven't lived in anything this nice for years, and I'd like to stay.*

The CD player worked, so Katherine sorted through CDs, most of which were to her liking, turned the volume down, kicked off her shoes, and lay back on the couch.

A ringing noise woke Katherine. It took several moments to orient herself and find the phone. As she put the receiver to her ear, she realized that she hadn't even known the phone was connected.

"Miss Duncan?" The pleasant female voice continued before Katherine could reply, "Kay said you rented the apartment. Is everything OK?"

"Uh, yes. Everything's fine. Who is this?"

"I'm Marlena Weathers. I'm calling from my cell phone downstairs because we have the same line. I didn't think about having the apartment phone made private, and it's too late for today, but tomorrow I'll have it taken care of. How do you want your listing?"

"I'd prefer to have it unlisted. Is that possible?" Katherine thought the voice was young, young and bossy. She also thought an unlisted number would thwart Pam for a while. "Yes," Katherine said with more authority, "unlisted. But, don't I have to take care of this sort of thing?"

"I'm really not sure, now that I think about it. I suppose someone has to go downtown to the phone company. Well, I'll leave it up to you, Miss Duncan." There was a pause, then, "To the right of the living room door there's a bookcase with louvered shutters that look like part of the paneling. If you like to read, have at it."

"Thank you," Katherine said.

"You're welcome." The line went dead.

Katherine sat staring at the receiver in her hand. So that was Miss Weathers of the illustrious ancestry, the rich Miss Weathers. *I already don't like her*, Katherine thought.

Streetlights were on, Katherine saw, and a dim light had gone on in the kitchen. *Probably a nightlight on a timer.* Realizing she was hungry, Katherine made a sandwich out of cold cuts and cheese, and downed a glass of milk. "Archie, where are you?" she whispered into the dark. "A bowl of your gumbo would have made my day."

The apartment was suffused with light when Katherine awoke. She sat up, yawning. There were moving shadows on the dormers as high winds passed through the branches of ancient trees next to the house. She had awakened for so many mornings to the swampy smell of sun on hot river sand that she was intrigued by the shadowy images dancing on crystal-clear glass. Also, she didn't hear birds or crickets or powerboats or the occasional far-off grunt of an alligator disturbed about something. The silence was almost eerie.

A warm shower and the thick, soft towels made her feel like a princess. She still could hardly believe her luck in finding a place to live that was not only squeaky clean, but clearly showed the hand of a decorator in every room. Her new home had the feel of an expensive, high-rise condo.

Katherine's list for the day began with the note to have a phone line installed, separate from the house phone. She had film for the printer, a conference to schedule with the university dean of public affairs, a chapter of text to be edited by the department of ornithology, and breakfast to eat.

As she pulled her car away from the curb, she saw a low-slung, red convertible in the narrow driveway on the side of the house opposite her stairway. "Good morning, Miss Weathers," she called softly. "And how are you this bright morning?"

Breakfast over and the phone company business behind her, she headed for the university. At least twice a month during her long vigil in the swamp, she had driven to New Orleans with film and scribbled text for the book, so she had no trouble finding her way to the lakefront. Her parking sticker gave access to the faculty lot. Feeling freer than she had in months, she breezed past students lounging on the stone steps.

She was more pleased than bothered by the few low whistles as she passed. Her bright auburn hair usually turned heads. Pam had been attracted to her because of it. Her hair, her slim figure, and her full breasts attracted more than Pam, but Pam had moved in on Katherine before anyone else gathered courage. Pam moved in and took control, and Katherine found herself stretching her legs over Pam's shoulders before they'd said much more than "Hi."

Katherine moved from building to building, taking longest with the ornithologist who insisted on lecturing her about the coloring of heron/egret legs and breeding plumage. Pleased that he had such an attractive audience of one, and with his eyes peering through Coke-bottle lenses, he dredged up everything he could recall that might be of use to Katherine when she began writing about her experience with the chicks. Dutifully, Katherine scribbled notes about black legs, yellow toes, and golden slippers, all the while wondering why she couldn't remember what she already knew and had observed in the swamp.

She told him, and several graduate students who wandered into the office, about the baby herons about to be swept away by the flood. They showed sympathy and understanding, which made Katherine's eyes water.

There was a note on Katherine's door. "Supper with me?" It was lettered on the inside scrap of a cereal box and signed "Marlena." Katherine was smiling grimly as she entered the kitchen. "Now it starts," she thought, "supper, then canasta or some other fool card game, and then shopping, then I'll never get rid of her. I knew this was too good to be true."

Not wanting to use the inside stairs, Katherine trudged down the outside stairs and rang the doorbell. She saw a figure through the frosted glass, but the person was indistinct. Katherine was not prepared in any way for the woman who greeted her.

"Hi, Miss Duncan. I'm Marlena. I hope you're here to tell me you'd be delighted to tear into a steak with me tonight. Steak, salad, maybe a baked potato if they don't burn to a crisp, and some of the great wine I found in the cellar." While the woman was talking, she guided Katherine into the house and shut the door. "If you're hungry now, I'll throw the steaks on the grill; otherwise, we can have a little wine and get to know each other."

Katherine had never been in an antebellum home that contained the original furnishings, as this one surely did. From where they stood just inside the door, Katherine could see gleaming spiral stairs at the end of an entrance hall that could have been used for a tennis court if there had been a net.

The woman touched Katherine's arm, breaking the spell. She had continued talking, but Katherine hadn't heard. "Well, which will it be, Miss Duncan?" she urged. "Supper or a tour?" Her touch was light on Katherine's arm, and Katherine heard a smile in the question.

"A tour, I think. I couldn't have imagined this from the outside, and I would love to see the rest." It occurred to Katherine that the offer of a tour was made facetiously, so Katherine now turned to look at her landlady to make sure. She looked and felt her heart thud as her senses took in the relaxed figure standing before her. Even in slacks and a loose silk shirt, the woman was regal. She was tall and slender, and her short, dark curls were natural. She was also amused, Katherine could tell.

"Then, would you like a glass of wine while we tour?" she asked finally. "I usually take at least an hour to do a thorough job."

"Please," Katherine managed at last, "I'm overcome. You actually live here?" With her hands she indicated the hall and the broad stairs and the ceiling that stretched for miles overhead.

"Yes, I lived here as a child, then again as an adult. I once lived in the upstairs apartment. Fact is, my aunt had the apartment made for me because I couldn't see spending my life in a museum, yet I wanted to be close to her. The apartment was a compromise."

"I should have such compromises." Katherine now looked directly at her new landlady, her glance taking in faint laugh lines around her clear, green eyes. *I'd like to touch her*, Katherine thought, wondering about the handsome, slightly masculine face.

The tour was thorough. Katherine gasped when she finally stood in the doorway to the formal dining room. Only in movies had she seen a table that would seat sixteen. Each of the table settings had enough glassware for an office picnic. Katherine was at ease now, so she asked, "Why is the table set? Are you having a banquet?"

"No, Aunt Helen kept it this way, so I left it. It takes the cleaning lady half a day just to keep the silver polished. I don't use this room; I keep it closed. I do my eating in the kitchen. You'll see."

As perfect as she seemed, Marlena Weathers was no cook. The potatoes were raw, the steaks overcooked, and the salad limp.

Marlena laughingly offered to go out for hamburgers, but a few more glasses of wine almost made the meal palatable.

"Tell me about yourself. I heard you were a photographer."

Katherine, trying almost frantically to cut a bite of steak and wishing she had a chainsaw, answered, "Yes, I had a studio in Mobile. I'm doing a coffee-table book now. I have a contract with the university to photograph seasonal changes in a swamp north of here."

"How interesting." Marlena filled the wineglasses again. "Do you have much more to do?"

"I'm finished with the seasons, except for some of the text. But I have dozens of rolls of a rookery that I'm going to add. I have approval, but I need expert advice so I won't describe a great blue and call it a cattle egret." The fate of the heron chicks plus many glasses of wine dissolved Katherine's usual reserve. "I am so sad about the babies," she sniffed.

"What babies?" Marlena leaned to touch Katherine's hand.

Katherine pushed her full plate aside and told a sympathetic Marlena the story of the chicks and the flood.

"There's nothing you can do, my dear." Marlena was shaking her head. "Nothing," she added sadly.

"I know. It's just so cruel." Katherine touched the napkin to her eyes and pushed back her chair. "I'd better go while I can still walk. Thanks for the meal. When I get settled I'll have you up to my place, OK?" She began stacking plates.

"No need for that." Marlena dismissed the cleanup with a flick of her hand. "You can use the inside stairs, if you like."

"Don't think so. The door is locked from my side."

"Well, good night then. I'm glad you came." Marlena kept her hand on Katherine's shoulder all the way to the front door.

A shell ridge had stopped most of the bags. The water wasn't deep enough for them to float over, and broken limbs had snagged those cruising along the bottom, safely anchoring them against the shells. Some of the bags' contents were light enough to float, and small floating things that escaped soon washed over the ridge. In clumps and singly, they bounced with the current, heading for the river. If the river crested higher, some of the intact bags could break loose and be pushed over the ridge. Like half-inflated balloons, they would float majestically toward their eventual destination, the shore of Lake Pontchartrain.

Chapter 4

Hungry, her head fuzzy from an unaccustomed amount of wine, Katherine made a sandwich and poured coffee into a mug with the initials EM imprinted on two sides. Thinking over the evening, she realized that Marlena had said very little about herself. "I'm the one who did the talking," Katherine said aloud to the cup. "I blabbed the whole time."

Sipping cautiously because the coffee was very hot, she wondered why a rental lease hadn't been necessary, and what Kay had meant when she said that Katherine was just the right person for the apartment. If Marlena ran three businesses, she probably knew what she was doing. Maybe she wanted someone who looked honest and wouldn't steal from downstairs since the apartment had easy access to the lower floors.

I'm going to guess, Katherine thought, *that Archie talked to her niece about me, told her everything she'd learned about me the year I stayed in her cottage, and then her niece called Marlena. There must be something about me that merits Marlena's approval. I wonder what it is.*

While taking her cup and plate to the sink, Katherine noticed that the printing on the cup didn't read EM, it was E plus M. So far, this was the only thing in the apartment that could be recognized as personal. The whole place, beautifully furnished as it was, was as impersonal as a hotel suite.

I'm too tired for a bath, Katherine thought as she searched for her gown. *I'll just brush my teeth and wash a bit.* The gown wasn't where she'd thrown it that morning, wherever that was, so she climbed, naked, into bed and fell instantly asleep.

A noise somewhere in the apartment awakened her. Throwing back the covers, she swung her feet to the floor and started to push off the bed before realizing she was not wearing a gown. The spread, which had been turned down earlier, was so huge that, when wrapped around her, part of it was still trailing on the bed when she reached the bedroom door.

"Is someone there?" Katherine called as she flipped the overhead light switch. A faint tapping sound answered.

Dragging the spread, she walked in the direction

of the sound, thinking it was someone on the landing outside the kitchen door. Peering through the glass, she asked, "Who's there?"

The landing was empty, but the tapping continued, faint and irregular, and now came from the bedroom. Katherine turned, entangling her feet in yards of soft fabric. "Damn!" she said through gritted teeth, stamping to free herself.

No one was in the bedroom. The tapping had stopped. Shrugging, Katherine climbed back into bed.

She had often spent long nights in the swamp waiting for first light so that she could photograph the marsh as it awoke. After listening to the splashing and grunting and screaming of those eating and being eaten in the darkness around her, Katherine wasn't about to be alarmed by what must have been a tree limb bouncing against the outside walls of her new apartment.

Archie had insisted Katherine carry a gun for those nights when Katherine stayed in the swamp alone, but the gun never got fired. It stayed snug in its waterproof pack under sandwiches and a thermos of coffee. Anyway, dense fog would have reflected a flashlight beam back into her face, so where was she to aim? The biggest danger, as Katherine saw it, was an accidental discharge through the bottom of the canoe, leaving her and some very expensive photographic equipment to sink out of sight in the dark water.

Katherine turned out the bedroom light, pulled the sheet around her and, wrapped like a cocoon, fell into a deep slumber.

* * * * *

The big mug from the night before had fitted her hand perfectly, so Katherine rinsed it and poured it full of fresh coffee. A long shower helped dispel a slight headache from the wine. Katherine dumped her duffel bag on the bed, digging the hair dryer from the heap of dirty clothes. Coffee in one hand, dryer in the other, she wandered into the living room and was pleased to see the apartment alight with sunshine, the east-facing window glass glittering with brightness.

As she was drying her hair, the phone rang. Not remembering that it could have been a call for her landlady, Katherine answered. Could Miss Duncan hang around until about noon? The man to install her new line would need to get into the apartment, and how many extensions does Miss Duncan want?

Waiting wouldn't be a hardship because Katherine wasn't one to eat a big breakfast. Toast, which she could make, and more coffee would easily hold her until her appointment at the university. There was nothing of interest on TV, so Katherine, curious, opened the bookshelf doors. "Aha!" she said aloud. "Now I know why I'm OK for this place." The shelves were full of lesbian novels, row after row.

Selecting one she hadn't read, Katherine sat on the couch and began reading. Twice, as the hours passed, Katherine refilled her cup. After the phone installer finished, Katherine selected her least wrinkled slacks and blouse for her appointment at the university.

On her way to the lakefront, she had a sudden thought. *Of course. Archie must have known I was gay all along, yet I hadn't even mentioned the* L *word during the time I lived in her cottage. Archie could see that I wasn't close with anyone; there were no letters and no calls. That last night when Pam showed up was the first time anyone visited me. It wouldn't be unlikely for Archie to figure I wasn't in a relationship, especially because of the way Pam tore out of the parking lot.*

My, my. Katherine grinned. *I must have a big* L *branded on my forehead after all.*

It was just called Cypress Swamp, Archie had said. There was no other name that she had ever heard. Katherine scrutinized the maps provided by the university librarian. The earliest maps showed almost the entire north shore of the lake ringed by swampland, all labeled *Cypress Swamp*. The area Katherine had photographed was a swamp; it had to be called something. *There simply isn't anyplace that doesn't have a name*, she thought as she tried to fit the river, the lake, and the highway into what she remembered of the area.

According to Archie, many, many years ago loggers had felled cypresses that were over a thousand years old. They had clear-cut an entire area of swamp that stretched for miles, leaving nothing but muddy water. Katherine saw on her maps that the places they cut had been given names. There was River Bend, Gator Slough, and Wilson's Cut. But, Katherine's swamp didn't seem to have a name at all, either on the old or the new maps.

"Is there a Louisiana historian on campus?" Katherine asked the librarian.

"I don't believe so." The woman frowned as she

tried to recall. Then she shook her head. "No, there isn't."

"I don't know what he's called, but Professor Leger is always talking about the Cajuns and how it was in the early days. He's supposed to be teaching sociology, but you can get him off the subject real easy." The speaker was a young man with a ponytail and buck teeth.

"What building?" Katherine asked, smiling. "It's worth a try," she explained.

Dr. Leger was alone in his tiny office. He looked up as Katherine peeped in the open door. "Yes, my dear?"

"I need the name of a swamp on the north shore, and the library maps aren't much help." Katherine paused, then said, "I was told you might be able to help me."

"Come in, come in." With an effort, Dr. Leger half stood, motioning to the only other chair in the office. "You're not a student?" he asked, his bald scalp reflecting the overhead light.

"No, I'm not." Katherine moved the chair closer to the desk and sat. "I'm photographing a swamp that doesn't seem to have its own name."

"If it's in an area northwest of the lake, then it's a piece of the Big Cypress Swamp that was cut off by a highway and a railroad and left for dead many, many years ago." With shaking hands he pulled a book off the shelf next to his chair. "Does that sound like the place?" he asked, riffling pages.

"I'm not from here." Katherine smiled. "I really don't have any idea. Seems to me that all swamps look alike once you're in them."

"Ah, no, my dear. We have an abundance of

marsh, and there are many differences." He pushed the large book across the desk, his finger pointing. "See, you can find the area by following existing roads and river pathways." His trembling finger circled an area south of the main interstate.

Katherine pulled the book closer and studied where his finger pointed. "Yes," she finally said, "I think that's it. At least it's probably close."

Dr. Leger sighed, his head nodding. "I know this region because I was born there. Years ago in the Big Cypress my father killed egrets and herons for their plumage, hundreds of them at a time. When I was young, it meant nothing to me, but now I regret the carnage." There was a look of genuine sorrow on his plump, red face. He shook his head, remembering.

"They seem to have made a comeback," Katherine offered.

"I hope so," he said, sighing. "Now, you wanted a name, didn't you? Well, the best I can do is *Railroad Swamp*. We called it that because the railroad owned it. Still does, I imagine. That was the local name for it and, because calling it that would identify the area, we used it. It was a part of Big Cypress until the railroad built straight through it."

"On maps it's still labeled Big Cypress Swamp," Katherine said in some dismay.

"Then you can call it that," Dr. Leger said, his lips puckered, his eyes bright behind thick lenses.

"So," Katherine said to her editor, "I still don't have a name for the book. Both maps and Dr. Leger agree that it was once a part of a larger area, but . . ."

"Why not Big Cypress, as you suggest? I like it."

"Because the original cypress swamp was destroyed years ago, and the area I photographed is what's left of it, and it isn't big anymore." Katherine shrugged. "Why don't we wait? I still have film to look at from the rookery and captions to write and . . ."

"In other words, put the title on hold?"

"We're ahead of schedule aren't we? It'll be a couple of weeks before the river goes down even if I decide I need more shots of the rookery. I can be busy finalizing a few things."

Katherine parked her car at the curb in front of her new home. She had grocery shopped, and now had several plastic bags crammed with edibles and cleaning supplies.

I'll have to make two trips, she thought, looking at the stairs. Purse hanging from her shoulder, a bag on each arm, she crossed the sidewalk, pushed the iron gate aside, and walked toward the side stairway.

"Wait! I have a better way."

Katherine turned; it was Marlena. "Morning," Katherine said. "Am I going to levitate, groceries and all?"

"Almost," Marlena answered. She was wearing dark slacks and a cream-colored pullover. Everything seemed fitted to show her slender figure, and for an instant Katherine looked at Marlena appraisingly from her head to her toe.

Marlena stood, hands by her sides, smiling under Katherine's scrutiny. "Yes?" she said softly, as if she could read Katherine's thoughts.

Katherine could feel the flush coloring her face. She could think of nothing to say.

"Wait," Marlena said. It took only a minute for her to gather the other grocery bags from the car. She led Katherine up the front steps and into the house. Katherine followed her into a sitting room just off the hall, and Marlena walked straight to a blank wall. She touched the wainscot, and part of the wall opened to reveal a metal cage.

"Here's your transportation upstairs," Marlena said.

"An elevator?"

Marlena nodded, stood aside so Katherine could enter first, then turned a brass key on the inside wall. They stood close as the cage began to rise. It was a smooth ascent. Katherine had no idea where it would end.

"Aunt Helen couldn't navigate the stairs after a while, so we had this installed. She liked for us to visit downstairs, but visiting upstairs was her way of getting out of the house without actually leaving it." Movement stopped, and Marlena pushed a handle that opened another door directly to the side of Katherine's bookcase.

"Milady." Gesturing to the living room with a sweep of her arm, Marlena stepped out. An astonished Katherine followed.

"Are there any more secrets I should know about?" Katherine put her bags on the kitchen table and indicated to Marlena to do the same. "I'm wondering when I'll touch the wrong thing and the floor will open under me."

Marlena's laugh was hearty. "No," she said, "I don't think so. I haven't used the elevator since Aunt Helen died, but you may whenever you're loaded down with groceries or whatever. Now, tell me where you want these." Marlena was holding two cans of asparagus.

"I haven't the faintest," Katherine answered. "I haven't even explored the cupboards yet. Why don't you leave that, and we'll have something cold? I have instant tea and Cokes."

"I designed this kitchen. I think I can remember where things will be convenient. Do you mind?" Marlena began opening cupboards and arranging canned things.

Katherine watched as Marlena, with brisk efficiency, placed the contents of each bag in a drawer or cupboard. She enjoyed watching Marlena reach for overhead shelves, and stoop to make use of under-counter space. As each bag was emptied, Marlena put it into a receptacle swinging on the inside of the door beneath the sink.

"I had this added because I never knew what to do with plastic bags. They seemed to reproduce overnight." Marlena's smile was warm, but not as warm as Katherine's scrutiny had made her.

Taking a deep breath, she said to Katherine, "If you have time, I'd like that tea now."

* * * * *

The rains had stopped farther north, and the Corps of Engineers opened a levee to help control flooding. The affected rivers in Louisiana slowed, shrank, then settled back into their accustomed pathways, leaving their banks scattered with debris. Whatever had floated across the swamp's shell barrier now floated in the river, bobbing toward the lake. Here and there, swirling eddies seized other floating things, carried them to the bottom and covered them with silt. Some eddies, however, moved whatever they carried directly to the sluggish, muddy water of the riverbank.

Chapter 5

"I haven't been up here in months," Marlena said. "It looks exactly the same."

"That's because I haven't done anything but put away a few clothes. I do have a pile of things to wash, if I can find a coin laundry." Katherine sipped her tea, noticing that Marlena had hardly raised her glass once.

"There's a place around the corner, about three blocks down. You could try there." Marlena's smile was open, friendly, but Katherine still sensed a touch of amusement that had nothing to do with the smile.

"Maybe later I'll take my things. Is there a dry cleaners, too?" *This is silly*, Katherine thought. *I can find my own cleaners; what I want is to know about her.*

"I think so, but I've had an idea. There's a washer and dryer downstairs. Feel free to use them whenever you need." Marlena put her untouched tea glass on a coaster and stood, looking down at Katherine. "Use the elevator."

Katherine nodded her thanks, watching Marlena walk toward the open elevator door. "You have beautiful hair," Marlena said as she stepped into the small cage and turned to face Katherine. "But you probably already know that."

Using a magnifying glass, Katherine was scrutinizing early color slides of the heron chicks. "They sure are cute," said the woman who was spreading the transparencies on the light table. "I'll bet you had fun in that swamp."

"It wasn't all sequins and feathers," Katherine said, shaking her head. "Downright scary at times is what it was, especially at night."

She was leaning over the light table, writing short comments on a lined tablet. "I can't see any reason to change a thing, Ruby. These are still the ones to enlarge, eight-by-ten as usual. Now, how about the ones I just brought in?"

Ruby placed a large package on the table. "I figured you'd want the same for these rolls, so I've already done the enlarging. I know you won't use them all, but I wanted to save time."

"Great, and you numbered them, too, I suppose?" Katherine spread the photos, corners touching, then picked them up one by one. Squinting, she held each at arm's length, studying the overall composition. Ruby stood behind her, leaning against a drafting table, her arms folded, and watching quietly as Katherine worked.

"You've done wonders with the colors. These are so true that I'm beginning to think you were there." Katherine was smiling now, her pleasure evident. "They're sharp, and I only wish we could use all of them." She paused, then handed two of the photos to Ruby. "Is that a man in the background here?" Her finger pointing, Katherine indicated the upper right corner of each photo.

Ruby frowned, then picked up the magnifier. The two photos were of the same area, identical in composition except for a slight difference in focal length. "Yes," Ruby said, "I think so. He seems to be standing behind something a darker shade of green than the cattails. Here, don't you think so?" She handed the photos and the glass to Katherine.

Katherine looked again for a long minute. "Let's blow up this one spot."

The enlargement did show a man in camouflage clothing standing next to a large, bald cypress, and he seemed to be looking straight at the camera. There was either a rifle or a stick in his right hand. The brim of a baseball cap shadowed his face.

"Damn," Katherine hissed. "I thought I saw movement at the edge of the rookery. I guess I was right." She turned to Ruby, her brown eyes flashing.

Slapping the photos down on the drafting table, she said, "Archie told me the place was full of harmless poachers. Ruby, this fellow looks menacing, doesn't he?"

"Sure does." Ruby nodded agreement.

"These were the last two frames on the roll, and I wasn't really setting up the shot. I just wanted clear foreground and hazy background, and I guess I didn't look carefully enough or I'd have seen him. I wonder if he's Archie's friend, Danny?"

"Send her the pictures."

"Good idea. I'll do that." Katherine remembered the feeling she experienced when that far-off movement had registered in the corner of her eye the last day in the swamp. Turning back to the rows of eight-by-tens, Katherine started noting her comments on their individual suitability.

It was dark when Katherine finished her careful scrutiny. Ruby had long gone. The place was empty, and Katherine's back was aching from hours bent over the table. *I'm hungry,* she thought, gathering her papers. *Do I want a burger, or should I eat some of the goodies I bought today?* The goodies won, and Katherine headed home.

Full of toasted cheese on wheat, Katherine set a steaming cup of coffee on the low table in front of the couch, curled her legs comfortably on the soft cushions, and began reading the last of the book she'd started earlier. As the chapters drew closer to the end, sex between the protagonist and her lover became frequent and sizzling. Katherine felt her heart quicken as the author's descriptions did what they were intended to do; she felt drawn into the love-making, a participant, as hands and mouth and soft flesh moved with an urgency that Katherine felt between her own legs.

"Pam," she breathed aloud. "Damn you!"

Faint knocking, and the sound of hushed laughter woke her. She sat up, still foggy from sleep. Holding her breath, she listened, but the sounds seemed to come from every direction.

I know it isn't someone on my landing; most likely it's coming from downstairs. Marlena must have company, and that elevator shaft is like a hollow tube. I'll bet I'm going to get every sound from downstairs when it's quiet at night.

Problem solved, Katherine slid under the sheet and was instantly asleep.

Dear Archie,

I've tried to call you, but you're never home. Have enclosed two photos I took on the last day. Remember I told you I thought I saw someone at the far edge of the rookery? Well, not only did I see, but I also photographed. Is this man the one you call Danny?

My phone number is unlisted, 555-4359. I haven't read about much more flooding along the river, so perhaps my baby chicks were spared. If you have a chance, take a look, and give me a call.

Another few lines, and Katherine placed letter and photographs in a large manila envelope, addressed, stamped, and ready for mailing later that day.

Marlena's car was in the drive. As Katherine pulled away from the curb, she saw Marlena and a young woman walking out the front door. They were laughing; Marlena's arm was around the woman's waist.

Aha. Katherine grinned. *Now I know what the whispers and tapping were. Marlena had her girlfriend for company last night. I don't know what they were doing, but making love would be my first guess. I'll probably have to get earplugs if I want a good night's sleep.* Katherine's grin widened.

After more hours over the light table, Katherine finished selecting prints. *If only,* she thought, *if only I had a title I'd be in great shape. I have to write a few words for each photo, and a description of the bird's lifestyle, but I'm sure I can get all the help I need at the university.*

Ruby, who had hovered nearby most of the time, asked, "Come eat a burger? You didn't have lunch, you know."

Katherine stretched, found that her back was now broken in several places, but answered, "Good idea." Gathering her rejects into a pile, she slid them into a folder that held other discarded prints. "I'll keep these, of course, Ruby. Mine isn't the only say, you know, and I've been overruled before."

"Harrumph! You know what I think about that,

don't you?" Ruby's displeasure was plain. "You took the pictures; you should be the one to make the selection."

"Ah, if only that were so," Katherine said.

Katherine described her new apartment to Ruby and also told her about the elevator and the door to the inside stairs. "My new landlady even offered me the use of her washer and dryer. In Mobile I have furniture in storage, but there's absolutely nothing I need for this apartment except food and cleaning supplies. Honestly, Ruby, it's perfect. And you should see the closet."

Ruby took the final bite of her cheeseburger. "One day you'll have to invite me over," she said, swallowing, "I'd like to meet your landlady, too. What's she like?"

Katherine took a deep breath. "Well," she said, "Marlena must be in her early thirties. She's slender, dark hair . . . dark, wavy hair, green eyes, and . . ." *No*, Katherine thought, *Ruby doesn't need to know Marlena's gay, or that I like her more than a little.* "She also owns three florist shops and isn't home much, although I did have supper with her, and I heard her downstairs last night." *I heard her making love*, Katherine thought, *and I wished it had been me instead of the blond woman I saw.*

Impressed, Ruby said, "You got lucky. There aren't many places like that. You're in a nice part of town, too."

* * * * *

Katherine put her portable typewriter on the desk in the small room that Kay had called an office. There was only the desk and one chair, but shelves covered two walls, and a waist-high window overlooked the street. Katherine unpacked the novels she had collected during the year at Archie's cottage. The paperbacks didn't fill half of one shelf.

Typing paper went into a desk drawer, assorted pencils and pens stood upright in a plastic glass on the desk, and erasers, paper clips, and an assortment of small change took up a few inches of space in the center drawer. *This is it,* Katherine thought, *I'll store stuff for each chapter on the shelves so all I have to do is reach for it.* She centered the typewriter on the desk, put the cover on a shelf, moved the phone so it would be available to her right hand, then stood back to admire her new workplace.

A computer would be helpful. Also I need more stamps and envelopes, a pair of scissors, some glue . . . Katherine sat at the desk and started making a list.

The phone rang. Katherine mouthed a silent prayer that it wasn't Pam. "Want to try again?" Marlena's voice was cheerful, and Katherine recognized it instantly.

"Supper?" she asked.

"My kitchen, half an hour. OK?"

It was more than OK with Katherine. "What can I bring?"

"Just bring yourself." The line went dead.

This time I'll use the inside stairs, Katherine decided as she dried her hands and ran a comb through her hair. As she watched her image turning side to side in front of the bedroom mirror, she felt unaccustomed excitement. "My dear," she said aloud to the mirror, "I think we're going on a date."

Marlena greeted her at the kitchen door. She was wearing an apron, and the room smelled of roasting meat. "My cleaning lady is the best cook in the world, and she fixed the meal. I was told to take it out of the oven" — Marlena looked at her watch — "this very minute."

Marlena carved thin slices and served both plates directly from the roasting pan. Potatoes, onions, and carrots cooked in delicious pot roast gravy made up the meal. "We have cheesecake for later," Marlena said.

Katherine was careful not to drink too much wine. She noticed that Marlena sipped a little at a time, too. "Whoa." Katherine laughed as she looked at her empty plate, "I've eaten way too much."

"I take that as a compliment, even if I didn't do the cooking." Pushing back her chair, Marlena said, "Let's go into the parlor. It's the only place in the house that has even partly comfortable furniture."

I'll bet your bed's comfortable, Katherine said to herself, *after all the whispering and going on I heard last night*. She followed Marlena, enjoying the play of silk across Marlena's slender shoulders and the enticing movement of her hips. *If you were to ask me right now, I'd say yes*, Katherine mused.

Marlena motioned Katherine to a small couch. They had to sit sideways in order to face each other. As Marlena kicked off her shoes and folded her legs under, she asked, "Are you with anyone?"

Katherine blinked. "No," she said faintly, surprised.

"That's hard to understand, Katherine. I think you could probably have anyone you wanted."

Katherine looked down at her clasped hands, unspeaking, her face turning pink.

"I'm talking about girlfriends, you understand. We're both lesbians, aren't we?"

Looking up, Katherine could only nod, her face now flaming.

"I'm not inviting you to bed, although I'd like that very much. I just want to know a little more about you." Marlena reached and covered Katherine's clasped hands with her own warm one. "Why are you alone?"

Katherine opened her mouth, but nothing came out.

"It's none of my business, but I am curious. I don't have anyone either, and you seemed to be going it on your own so I thought I'd ask." Smiling, Marlena gave a little shrug.

Unaccustomed to such bluntness, Katherine could only stare. Then she remembered why she was alone. "I was with someone in Mobile," she said hesitantly. "We weren't getting along, so when I agreed to do the swamp photographs I stored my things, packed my clothes, and left. I didn't leave a forwarding address, either."

Katherine also remembered why she and Pam hadn't been getting along, but she didn't see that it was necessary to tell Marlena. Also, she recalled that she and Pam had been naked, clawing at each other within hours of first meeting. *But*, Katherine thought, *Pam is that kind of person. Pam takes without asking, and that excited me at first.*

Marlena gave a short laugh that was totally without humor. "We're alike, I think. I caught my lover of eight years in bed with another woman, so I packed her things and booted her out that same day. It was hard to do because I loved her, but . . ."

Katherine asked, "You were living upstairs, weren't you?"

"Yes." There was such sadness in Marlena's green eyes that Katherine leaned and touched Marlena's arm.

"Is that why you're not living there now?"

"Yes. There were too many memories." Marlena put her hand over Katherine's hand. For a few moments, they sat touching, each remembering.

The river was returning to normal except for debris still floating or lodged around the newly formed sandbars. Small pleasure craft took to the water again. Those who owned camps along the river were pleased to see that the water, which had risen higher than most boat docks, had not invaded their cabins, which were raised on sturdy pilings. They began airing out, nailing back, and raking debris into the water so that the current would carry it away. Under an adult's watchful care, small children began swimming and splashing in the shallows. The water was warm, the current was predictable, and the river was friendly again.

Chapter 6

"I enjoyed dinner, especially the cheesecake." Katherine turned to look at Marlena, who was climbing the wide, inside stairs beside her. They reached Katherine's door.

"I'll have to tell Miss Cora you said that. She'll be very pleased. When Aunt Helen was alive, Miss Cora cooked every day. Now she only does special things for me when I ask."

"Well, dinner was certainly special." Katherine opened the door. "Next time I'll cook," she promised.

"We're friends?" Marlena asked unexpectedly.

Nodding, Katherine said, "Yes." *And*, she thought, *I wish we were going to be a little more than friendly*. She almost reached out, but she stopped the gesture in time. She smiled at Marlena and nodded goodnight.

Later, she found it impossible to get to sleep, her thoughts a jumble. *I was doing fine at Archie's until Pam found me, and I know there's no future with Pam. Now I have a crush on Marlena, except I think she's way out of my league. Anyway, Marlena lied when she said she was alone. I know what I heard coming from downstairs, and she certainly wasn't doing it by herself.*

Marlena, lying propped on pillows in her huge bed downstairs, was also thinking. *I got rid of Eva when she started screwing that frowsy tramp, then I fell for Millie, who was in love with someone else and certainly didn't want me. Now I'm thinking of luring my tenant into bed. I wonder what it would be like?* Sighing, Marlena slid beneath the covers, and drifted into sleep.

The whispering began during the wee hours of the night. When Katherine opened her eyes, the small kitchen light enabled her to guess at the outlines of bedroom furniture, and faraway streetlamps faintly lit the dormer windows, so she slid from the bed and walked barefoot across the living room to the elevator door.

"I have no business being an eavesdropper," she said to herself as she put her ear to the wooden panel. Yes, the sound was coming from downstairs, and, yes, two women were whispering, probably while making love. The sounds were those Katherine knew from experience. Soft gasps and gentle moans increased in intensity until, finally, cries hushed as passion crested.

Katherine's eyes were squeezed shut. She had felt her own breathing quicken as the sounds climaxed. *Good God,* she thought, *it was so clear I could almost feel Marlena touching me.*

There were no more sounds from downstairs. The apartment was silent as Katherine huddled on the sofa, sleep forgotten, memories crowding for attention.

Archie called as Katherine was on her second cup of coffee.

"Hi, sweetie. Just opened your letter."

"That was fast," Katherine laughed. "I just mailed it."

"Well, I'm only fifty miles as the crow flies, you know. I'm glad you're safe and settled, but Kay called me the day you rented your new apartment, so I knew you were OK. How did you like my niece?"

"She was very helpful. I liked her," Katherine

said. "Now, my friend, I don't guess you've had time to get to the rookery, supposing that you can even make your way in there."

"Danny took me yesterday afternoon, and guess what!"

Katherine took a deep breath. "The babies are gone?"

"No, sweetie, they're OK. Feet a little wet, maybe, but as hungry as ever. And are they growing!"

Katherine could feel her body relax; the relief was palpable. "Archie, I'm so glad to hear that. You don't know how often I've thought about those babies."

"Well, I'll keep my eye on them as best I can. There are so many babies this year, the place is almost crowded. Your two will come back, you know, to raise their own family. We won't be able to tell them from the rest, but that's OK."

"Did you look at the pictures?"

"Sure did. Don't think I know the man, though. The pictures aren't very clear."

"I can do some computer enhancing, and I'll send you what I get." Katherine paused. "I don't have a clue why it seems important, but have another look, please. And," Katherine continued, "I haven't even asked you about the high water. Is your place OK?"

"My garden washed away, but that's about all. Danny helped me move the canoes and raise the stuff in the shed. Also, Betty and Nina send their regards. They're leaving Saturday next."

"Tell them hello, and get their address so I can send them an autographed copy."

"Sure will, honey. You take care now."

Katherine was smiling as she hung up. She pictured the heron chicks alive and well and growing.

They probably even had a few real feathers by now. Katherine needed a happy picture to erase the memory of Marlena and whoever having great sex in the middle of the night. *I will not listen again*, she promised herself.

Eric, six and growing fast, scooped something out of the sandbank. His sister, four, was digging wet sand out of the hole she had dug at the river's edge. Eric examined his treasure, recognizing it for what it was. "I'm the doctor," he said gleefully to his sister. "I'm going to give you a mosquito bite, and you'll feel better, see." One chubby hand grasped his sister's arm while the other curled tightly around his find. He stabbed the pointy end into his sister's flesh. She screamed.

Katherine worked with her editor until early afternoon. After reading and rereading, writing and rewriting, Katherine was sure of the text for the seasonal changes. Text and photos agreed; the seasons were documented, and they flowed from one to the other as nature moved inexorably from birth to rebirth. Bare branches put forth leaves; seeds for the next generation took their place within the canopy of green; colors changed; leaves crisped; and once more bare branches awaited the coming of spring. Katherine had caught every nuance on film.

I can make pretty good meatballs and spaghetti, Katherine acknowledged to herself later as she walked the aisles of the supermarket. *I'll invite Marlena for tomorrow night. I like playing with fire.*

While she was unpacking groceries, she heard tapping coming from the living room. *Is Marlena at it again?* she wondered as she crossed the carpet. This knock was brisk, however, and was coming from the stairway door. "Yes?" Katherine called.

"I'm having leftovers, Katherine. Want to share?"

"Ah." Katherine hesitated. "I'd like that." *But*, she thought as she opened the door, *can I look her in the face after hearing what I heard last night?*

"Hi, neighbor. Does a hot roast beef po'boy for supper sound good?" Marlena's smile was broad and inviting. Katherine smiled back.

"That sounds great, neighbor. How soon do you want me?"

Marlena arched her eyebrows, her laugh acknowledging Katherine's double entendre. "Whenever you're ready," she said. "How about now?"

Blushing, Katherine nodded. "I have ice cream," she offered.

They ate in the kitchen. Marlena carved slivers of roast, and made po'boys three inches thick with gravy dripping and mayonnaise oozing. They did more eating than talking, and Marlena groaned when she pushed back her chair. "I've eaten too much again," she said, "and I have gravy all down my front."

Katherine giggled. "I know. Look at me."

"Let me wipe that for you," Marlena said. She dipped the edge of a napkin in her water glass and began wiping the front of Katherine's blouse. Her movements were slow and sensuous, and Katherine's nipples responded to the touch of Marlena's hand.

Katherine raised her gaze and found Marlena's eyes inches away.

"That's enough," Katherine said softly.

Slowly, Marlena leaned away. She was aware of Katherine's involuntary response. "That wasn't planned, you know. But I don't think you minded, did you?"

Katherine was statue still, her heart beginning to gallop as she shook her head. "No," she said honestly, unable to meet Marlena's eyes. "No," she said again.

"I want to make love to you," Marlena said, her voice a whisper. "I've felt this way since we first met." Gently, she lifted Katherine's chin so that they were eye to eye again. She leaned with glacier slowness and touched Katherine's lips with her own. It was a tender kiss. Marlena's lips were soft, and Katherine opened her mouth to the taste of Marlena's tongue.

During their lovemaking, Katherine realized that the sounds they were making could not reach the elevator shaft. It was two rooms away. Marlena and whoever would have to have been lying on the floor directly in front of the elevator door. The thought was fleeting. At that moment Katherine's body was arched, racked with orgasmic spasms, her breath a gasp of ecstasy, so the brief thought vanished like feathers in a windstorm.

Marlena's whisper woke Katherine. It was morning. "I have to go now. You can stay in bed as long as you want. Miss Cora isn't coming today. I'll be home sometime around two o'clock, after a noon wedding downtown."

Katherine felt Marlena's lips on her forehead. She moved her head so that Marlena's lips were in reach. Marlena's mouth was sweet, and Katherine held their heads together with her hand. A moment passed, and when Marlena's hand found Katherine's breast, the kiss deepened.

Katherine put her arms around Marlena's shoulders. "Love me before you go," she said. Her mouth opened again, and Marlena's tongue dipped between Katherine's lips. Katherine felt the room's coolness as Marlena threw back the covers, but the sudden chill lasted only a few seconds. Marlena's warm hand caressed Katherine's naked flesh; her lips sucked Katherine's raised nipples, teeth gently nibbling, and Katherine cried aloud when Marlena's fingers slid through moisture, piercing Katherine to the core.

Katherine gathered her clothing, which was crumpled on the floor next to Marlena's bed. She walked past the giant armoire next to the bathroom door, stopping to look at herself, front and back, in the mirror. *Except for this silly grin and the stickiness between my legs, I seem much the same. I am not, however, the same Katherine.* This thought pleased her. *I'll use Marlena's john, but I'll go shower upstairs where my stuff is,* she thought sensibly.

Naked and carrying her clothing, she climbed the carpeted stairway to her apartment. The door was unlocked on both sides, and Katherine pulled it open with her free hand.

Pam was waiting, her hands on her hips, a hateful grin on her face. "Had a nice night, love?"

Katherine stopped as if she had run into a tree. "How did you get in here?" she asked, unmindful of her nakedness. Pam had seen her naked many times.

"Have you ever seen a lock I couldn't open?" Pam moved a step closer.

Katherine took a step back. She covered what parts she could with her clothes, dropping a shoe. Pam took another step, picked up the shoe, and, at the same time, tore the clothing from Katherine's unresisting hand. "You know I like you buck naked, don't you girl?" Pam flung the clothes behind her, and with snakelike speed, grabbed Katherine's arms. Her grip was strong and hurtful, and Katherine tried to twist away.

Standing naked while a fully clothed person assaulted her defeated all of Katherine's efforts to free herself. With her arms caught, she couldn't even fight back.

Pam pushed her down on the sofa, both strong hands pressing Katherine's shoulders into the smooth fabric. "You've been fucking someone, haven't you? I can smell it, bitch."

Katherine pulled at Pam's hands, and she began kicking. Pam's grip loosened. She stood, turning to face the door.

Marlena, her cell phone at her ear, was giving an address to someone on the other end of the line. Her face was as calm as stone, her voice soft, steely. She looked at Pam. "The police will be here in three minutes. If you want your freedom, get the hell out of here right now. Out," she said with a coldness that made Katherine shiver. "Out, now!" She hadn't moved from the doorway.

Pam turned. Without a word, she walked through the kitchen, opened the door to the stairway landing, and left, closing the door behind her.

Now Marlena moved. She knelt at the couch, her face concerned. "Are you hurt?"

Katherine felt giggles starting. She felt silly lying there. "No," she said, trying to suppress the choking laughter that threatened to explode from her throat. "God, no!" Unconscious of her nakedness and the tears that streamed, she put her arms around Marlena. "I was so afraid." She began sobbing.

Later, downstairs, while sipping tea, Marlena said, "Good thing I had to come back for some papers and heard noises through the open stairway door. Who was she, and what happened?"

Katherine told Marlena about Pam. In jerky sentences, she explained Mobile. "I don't know why I let it happen, but Pam came on to me so strong that even though she practically raped me I enjoyed every minute and wanted more. We didn't live together. I had a photo shop with an apartment upstairs, and she'd come by to have sex." Katherine shivered at the memory.

For a moment, Katherine couldn't find words, then she continued, and her voice was a whisper, causing Marlena to lean closer.

"We went at it like we were starving, day and night. One day I had a shoot and had to tell her no. She flew into a rage and slammed me all around my shop . . . not for the first time, either. I packed up and left, sold my place by telephone, and here I am."

Marlena stroked Katherine's cheek. "I won't let her hurt you."

"I don't know how she found me, or even why." Katherine slowly shook her head. After a pause she said softly, "I enjoyed last night. Will what happened spoil . . . ?"

"Spoil what we had? No, Katherine. In fact, I feel that day-and-night starving, too, when I'm with you."

"Were you really calling the police?"

"No, but if she hadn't gone I would have."

Katherine put her empty glass on the table and pushed back her chair. "I need a bath. Will you stay with me while I dress?"

Officer Tangy of the river patrol looked at Eric with what he hoped was a friendly smile. "Now," he said, kneeling, "where did you get this?" Eric clung to his mother's leg.

"Over there." He pointed to the sandbank. "I found it," he explained.

Officer Tangy rose. "Well, ma'am," he said to Eric's mother, "let's get this young lady to the hospital. Our boat is faster, so you and the little lady will go ahead with us. Dad, you can follow in your boat."

Chapter 7

They were both asleep; Katherine's head was on Marlena's shoulder, and her hand curved around Marlena's breast. They breathed quietly, bodies stilled. Upstairs, Katherine could occasionally hear the roar of the transit bus if it stopped at the corner across from the house. Downstairs, in the silence of walls over a foot thick, no street sounds penetrated. Katherine turned to lie on her back and, in that moment of near wakefulness, heard soft whispering. She lay for a moment, unmoving, wondering if she were dreaming. Not even the ticking of a clock disturbed the silence. There were only the tender sounds of two women; their whispering came from far away, and was not clear enough for Katherine to distinguish words.

She raised herself on her elbows, heart thudding. Marlena was definitely next to her, snoring gently. Marlena could not possibly be making love with some unknown person and still lie snugged at Katherine's side. "Wake up," Katherine hissed in Marlena's ear, poking Marlena's arm. "Wake up!"

"Ummm." Marlena reached for Katherine.

"No," Katherine said louder, "wake up!"

"What?" Marlena said. "Is it morning?"

"Be quiet and listen," Katherine whispered. They were both very quiet for several minutes, Katherine because she listened intently and Marlena because she had gone back to sleep. Finally Katherine struggled to a sitting position. "Damn," she said, poking Marlena again. "It's stopped."

"What stopped?" Marlena mumbled, yawning.

"What I heard, the two women . . . oh, hell, get up and we'll have coffee. I have to tell you something."

At the kitchen table, more awake now, Marlena said, "I don't believe a word of that."

"It's true as surely as I'm sitting here. I hear them every night. I honestly thought you were down there having an orgy with your girlfriend. I thought you were lying when you told me you didn't have anyone because I could hear you having someone just an hour or so later."

"On the floor in front of the elevator shaft?" Marlena rolled her eyes. "Give me some credit, Katherine. I am not into floor games. I like comfort."

"You're teasing, I know, but I have been hearing

something. Can you honestly say you've never heard a thing?"

"I can honestly say that." Marlena was nodding. "In bed tomorrow night, let's listen. I may have to restrain you physically because of the noise you make." Marlena tapped on the table with her index finger. "I'm thinking a towel stuffed in your mouth will do the trick." She arched one eyebrow in question.

"The trick will be for you to keep your hands to yourself. Suppose I sleep in my own bed tomorrow night?"

"Fine with me, as long as I'm in it with you." They started laughing, the first unrestrained joy the old mansion had heard in a long time.

"Do you have anything to do today that can't be put off until tomorrow?"

Katherine added jelly to her toast and took a bite before answering. "I have plenty to do, but I suppose it'll wait. Why? Do you have something in mind?"

"This is end-of-the-month time, and I really need to see my accountant. We usually go together to each store and do tax things, and I have to sign checks and stuff." Marlena grimaced. "It's the part I hate, but I do enjoy the money. It keeps me from having to work. I'll buy your lunch if you come with me."

Katherine was smiling. "I'd like nothing better than to spend the day with you. But won't I be in the way?"

"I'm usually foaming at the mouth after a couple

of hours trying to make things balance. Being with you will keep me focused."

And being with you will keep me horny all day, Katherine thought. "OK," she said, "let's do it."

The manager at the Canal Street store was waiting with a stack of papers. "You won't have any problem with these figures," she said. "I'm happy to say that we balanced to the penny this month."

The accountant, whose name was Harold, looked over each page. "These are fine," he informed Marlena. "Sign the checks and we'll head for town."

The three of them jammed into the one seat of Marlena's tiny foreign convertible. Marlena zipped them through traffic and pulled into the back parking lot of her Saint Charles Avenue store in just under twenty minutes.

Harold was grinning as he tried to rake his sparse hair back into place. "This is your fastest time ever, Marlena. And we didn't run over a soul."

"Is that what Marlena does? I had my eyes closed most of the way." Katherine was also trying to tame her hair, which the wind had whipped in all directions.

"I'm in a hurry," Marlena said, slamming the car door. "I have plans for lunch."

Katherine followed them into the small office, winding her way between gladioli standing in cans of water. "These are going to be white when they open, aren't they?" Katherine remarked to Marlena. "Are they for something special?"

"We have a big society wedding next Sunday, all white flowers, and these glads are for the church. I can only hope they're going to be white because that's what we ordered." Marlena pointed to a chair. "Sit here next to me," she said.

Katherine waited as Harold and Marlena discussed daily balances and past-due accounts. The store seemed very busy to Katherine. The phone rang constantly. Several women were working at a wide counter, wiring wooden picks on flower stems, and arranging the bright blooms as funeral wreaths.

One of the women came to the office door and asked Marlena, "Do you want to send something from you? I know you knew His Honor personally."

Marlena looked up. "Glad you thought of that. Yes, but not too big. I wouldn't want to make any of our customers look chintzy."

Finally, when the last check was signed, Marlena said, "Harold, I'm going to drop you at the Magazine Street store, and Katherine and I are going to lunch. Do what you can there, and I'll get back as soon as I can."

"Where are we going now?" Katherine asked. She knew enough about New Orleans to recognize that the car was headed for the lakefront.

"I have a surprise for you," Marlena explained. "It's a very, very exclusive club for women only. I thought you'd enjoy eating there."

The house was huge, two stories, set back from Lakeshore Drive. A tall, iron fence guarded the entire parking area. Katherine didn't see a sign, but since it was a private club she figured it probably didn't need one. The parking lot was full, mostly with Lexus, Lincolns, BMWs, and Cadillacs.

They entered at the back and walked down a long hall. At the end was a wide stairway. Marlena took Katherine's hand, leading her through an arched opening into a large room with café chairs and small, sidewalk tables arranged around what was obviously a dance floor. The only light came from candles glowing in glass containers at each table's center.

After they were seated, a young woman brought ice water to their table and asked for their order. Marlena didn't need the menu — iced tea, ham-and-cheese on French, potato salad. When the waitress left, Marlena clasped Katherine's hand. "Supper here can be delicious and very elaborate," she said. "Lunch is mostly a token meal for those who come to go upstairs. Like us."

"Upstairs?" Katherine echoed. "What's upstairs?"

When their meal was finished, Marlena didn't linger. She stood and, taking Katherine's hand, walked to the broad staircase Katherine had seen in the hall. Mystified, Katherine let herself be led to the top of the stairs. Another hall, with closed doors right and left, seemed to stretch the length of the house. Marlena led Katherine to one of the doors. "Here we are," she said, opening the door to reveal a luxurious bedroom.

Katherine followed Marlena to the center of the room. The first thing she noticed was the mirrored ceiling over the bed. There was also a bathroom with a Jacuzzi and mirrored walls. "What is this place?" she asked, although the bed and private bath were clues.

"If I had been making the sounds you thought you heard, I would have been here. This is where I do my lovemaking, Katherine, not in the bedroom at home. This is why what you heard couldn't have been me."

"But," Katherine reminded her, "we've certainly made use of your bedroom."

"And we will again." Marlena started opening Katherine's blouse. "After Eva, I moved downstairs. It didn't seem right to bring anyone into Aunt Helen's house, either before she died or after. She would have understood because she was gay, but I just couldn't." Marlena reached around to unsnap Katherine's bra. She put it and the blouse on a chair next to the bed. "Now," she said, "your slacks."

Katherine willingly kicked off her shoes and stepped out of her slacks. Removing her briefs, she turned into Marlena's arms.

"Did you lock the door?" she asked.

That night Marlena heard the whispering, too. "My God," she said. "Where is it coming from?"

"You know this house better than I do. Where do you think?"

"Get up," Marlena ordered. "We'll find out."

Tiptoeing because it seemed the right thing to do, they moved out of the bedroom, crossed the sitting room, and stood in front of the elevator door. "It's no louder here," Marlena said.

"No," Katherine whispered, "I think it's coming from all over. But how's that possible?"

"May I say something outrageous?" Marlena

asked. Not waiting for Katherine's answer she said, "One of them sounds like Aunt Helen."

"But isn't she dead?"

"Yes, Katherine, I know that. I didn't say it was Aunt Helen, just that it sounded like her." Marlena turned and, pulling Katherine by the arm, walked through to the kitchen. She flipped the light switch, and both blinked at the sudden brightness. Going to the cupboard, Marlena selected a bottle of red wine. "We need this, I think."

They sat facing each other. Marlena poured wine. Katherine bit her thumbnail. An undercounter fluorescent light began blinking, making a tiny tinkle each time the tube dimmed. They both stared.

Marlena broke the silence. "I was raised mostly in this house," she said.

Katherine waited for more.

"I know the noise wasn't rats in the wall because the walls are solid. There aren't any rats under the floors, either. The bug man comes on a regular basis. He'd find something if there was something to find." Marlena paused. "The sounds we heard, at least what I heard, seemed to be somebody whispering to somebody else, and then that person whispering an answer."

Katherine nodded solemnly. "Yes," she said.

"We should search, don't you think? Some of the upstairs rooms haven't been opened for a long time. There just hasn't been any reason to use them, especially when Aunt Helen couldn't get around very much." Marlena was quiet, thinking. "I don't have a gun," she said finally. "I do have a baseball bat, and there are knives here in the kitchen."

Katherine was frightened by Marlena's statement.

She had not thought about needing a weapon. "Why not call the police? I've heard the noise more than once, so whoever or whatever —"

"You mean it could be somebody living here in the house that I don't know about?" Marlena shook her head. "I doubt that. Let's go back to the bedroom, get dressed, and start searching upstairs. We'll even look through your apartment.

"My new kitchen lock would certainly keep anyone from coming in up there. Even Pam couldn't break in that way, but we should search thoroughly, I think." Katherine pushed her wineglass to the center of the table, then held out her hand to Marlena.

"We did hear something, didn't we?" Marlena needed confirmation.

"Yes," Katherine said. "Now we'll find out what it was." *If I can spend the night in a tiny canoe with the possibility of snakes for company and who knows what else lurking within arm's reach, I can certainly look for two women who whisper in the night*, Katherine thought. *Or for a tree branch raking a windowpane*, she added sensibly.

Flashlights were unnecessary because there was electricity throughout the house, but they each carried one anyway. They looked under beds, beneath tables, behind curtains, and in the huge armoires. Unnecessarily, they even opened small cupboards to peer inside. Each room was thoroughly searched.

At first, in Katherine's apartment, as they moved from room to room they spoke in normal tones. After making sure the elevator cage was downstairs, Marlena flipped a wall switch, and said quietly, "The only way this thing will move is if someone turns it on from this switch. It can't be operated from downstairs now."

Taking her cue from Marlena, Katherine whispered. "When we go downstairs, let's make sure my door is locked behind us. That way we will have isolated this part of the house." She hesitated at the closed elevator door, listening, but there was no sound.

After they locked Katherine's door from the downstairs side, they moved slowly down to the second-floor landing, their steps noiseless on the carpet. Marlena motioned with her head, and they went to the right side of the hall, neither speaking. Door after door was opened and the room searched, then the door was locked from the hall side. They moved quietly, and after making sure a room was empty, they stood motionless, listening.

Finally, after the first floor had been searched, they walked back to the kitchen. Marlena poured wine, saying, "There isn't anyone in this house who shouldn't be in this house. What we heard was the wind moving a tree branch somewhere. You know how old this place is. It stands to reason there would be some creaking and groaning, don't you think?"

Katherine could only nod in agreement. She looked at the kitchen clock. "It's after four, and I do have some computer stuff to do for Archie. Let's go back to bed."

Later, in the dark bedroom, two pairs of eyes stared at the ceiling. Neither Katherine nor Marlena believed the tree branch theory.

Chapter 8

With Ruby's help, Katherine worked on the two prints from the rookery. She did not recognize the man who had watched her, but enlarged, his features were finally clear. She packaged two eight-by-tens for Archie and dropped them in the mail on her way back to the apartment. *I'm too sleepy to do anything but take a nap*, she decided, opening the kitchen door.

The bedroom, brightened by afternoon sunlight beaming through the dormer windows, was comfortably cool. Katherine undressed except for her briefs and slid beneath the sheet. Her eyes closed, and sleep came almost immediately.

The ringing of the bedside telephone awakened her. Without opening her eyes, she fumbled the receiver to her ear. There was no sound from the other end. Katherine listened without speaking, and, finally, the caller hung up. Awake, and certain that Pam now had her unlisted number, she gritted her teeth.

I haven't heard the last of her, Katherine thought wearily. *She's going to hound me until she gets what she wants, but what could she possibly want? Sex? Pam is crazy to believe I'd ever sleep with her again. We were never in love*, Katherine reflected. *We had sex, yes, but I didn't love her. I only wanted what she did to me in bed. It was never making love; it was just having sex.*

Katherine thought about those wild times. At first, just seeing Pam coming through the shop door was enough to make moisture ooze between Katherine's legs, and Pam would start tearing at Katherine's clothes before they'd said hello. Many times Pam wouldn't wait for Katherine to undress, and Katherine would feel Pam's hand snaking under briefs or bra, reaching for the sensitive places that ached to be touched. Their mouths joined in lip-bruising kisses, and Pam's thrusting would deepen to the point of pain. Katherine often tried to pull away but, pressed flat against whatever they were using, she could only squirm.

In spite of Pam's roughness, or because of it, Katherine's orgasms were explosive. *But I know why*, Katherine thought. *For two years I threw up after sex with my husband. I was never aroused, not once, and all sex did was make me lose sleep and dirty the sheets. I've wanted sex with a woman all my life; I just didn't know it.*

Her nap interrupted by the phone and by the hateful memories that crowded her senses, Katherine dressed and went to the kitchen to begin making meatballs for spaghetti. *I'll make an avocado salad, and we'll have wine and candlelight.* She smiled, pleased to think that she would spend the evening and entire night with Marlena.

Marlena was pleased, too. When she appeared at Katherine's inside door, a large bouquet of bright flowers was in her hand. "I hope you have something big enough to hold these," she said. "Somehow I couldn't stop adding."

They kissed, embracing for a long moment. Marlena broke the spell. "What do I smell, meatballs and spaghetti?" she asked.

"I promised to cook for you, didn't I? Well, tonight's the night if you have time."

"Madam, I'll always have time to dine with you. In fact, I'm starving, so when do we eat?" Marlena saw the candles, the wineglasses, and the table set for two. "You've gone to a lot of trouble, but I'll make it worth your while," she promised.

Katherine put the flowers in the center of the small table, then moved the bouquet to the kitchen counter because it blocked their view of each other and the lighted candles made it a fire hazard. Katherine turned off the overhead light, and they ate with the candle glow causing shadows to flicker on the kitchen walls. "I thought this would be romantic," Katherine explained.

Marlena paused in mid-bite. "You know I'm wooing you with flowers, don't you? I want us to be more than friends, Katherine."

Katherine felt heat rising to her face. "Marlena," she began seriously, "you don't know enough about me. I haven't been . . . I haven't been entirely honest."

"I know about your friend Pam. What else is there? You're a murderer, maybe?"

"No." Katherine smiled sadly, shaking her head. "But I've been married. Pam was my second affair with a woman, and now I want you sexually the way I wanted her. But I don't know that I'm a lesbian, even though I feel desire so strong I can barely breathe when I'm around you." Katherine was twisting her napkin, eyes brimming.

"Having been married doesn't mean a thing, Katherine. Probably half of my lesbian friends are widowed or divorced. I'm just lucky that I knew almost from birth that I am a lesbian." Marlena was choosing her words. "Because of the way society is set up, some women don't find out until after they're committed to a man, and then it's often too late. But now that you know, you won't have to live a lie the rest of your life."

Katherine didn't touch the tears that dripped from her chin. She wanted Marlena to hear the truth. "I didn't even try to resist Pam. I had no idea where the relationship was going, only that I didn't want it to stop."

"You're blaming yourself for something you couldn't help. I don't care about a husband. I don't care about Pam, either. I know how tender and loving you are in bed, and I know we please each other." Marlena moved her plate and the candles so that she could reach for Katherine's hands. "Please stop crying," she begged. "Calling yourself by one title or the other won't change the feelings nature has given you."

"I feel so ashamed," Katherine sobbed.

"You're being foolish. There's nothing to be ashamed of. We've only known each other for a few days. You hadn't time to tell me your whole life history. But now you've told me, and I still want you physically, so let's go sit on the sofa and make out."

Katherine started laughing. Once on the sofa, she dabbed her eyes and clasped Marlena's outstretched hands. They sat close, touching from thigh to shoulder. With exaggerated care, Marlena put her arm around Katherine. 'S OK?" she asked quietly.

Katherine nodded.

"Nibble your ear?" Marlena whispered.

Katherine nodded again.

"Do more?" Marlena suggested, her voice soft.

"Yes, more," Katherine answered, rising. "Much more," she added as they walked to the bedroom.

A new awareness seemed to motivate Katherine. She undressed Marlena, moving with such deliberate slowness that Marlena began helping. "Don't," Katherine ordered, pulling down bra straps. "I want to undress you myself."

A naked Marlena had to lie on the bed, watching, as Katherine stripped. By the time Katherine knelt, one knee between Marlena's outstretched legs, Marlena was desperate to be touched. She held out her arms. "Please," she said. "Please."

"All in good time," Katherine promised. Slowly, oh so slowly, Katherine began touching Marlena. She touched with her hands, her tongue. She pressed her body into Marlena's warmth and felt Marlena's heart thudding, breath rasping.

"Katherine, please." Marlena's hips were writhing. She was very ready. Katherine touched Marlena's wetness with her fingers and stroked the velvet flesh within. As Marlena gasped, Katherine settled her mouth against throbbing flesh and pressed her fingers into slippery darkness.

It seemed to Marlena that her entire body was lifting off the bed, held in suspension by Katherine's busy fingers and by Katherine's lips and tongue moving in the moisture that gushed between Marlena's legs. When the spasms began, Marlena found herself grunting to the rhythm of Katherine's hand. Then she gave a breathless sob and relaxed, Katherine still within her.

"I've never done that before." Katherine pressed her mouth to Marlena's breast. "I liked fucking you very much. I like tasting you, feeling my tongue inside you, feeling you come."

"If you keep talking like that, I'll have to come again." Marlena moved Katherine's head so that the other nipple was within reach. "For a minute there I thought I was flying."

They were still, except for the movement of Katherine's tongue on Marlena's hardening nipple. "Much more of that," Marlena warned, "and you'll be in trouble. Anyway, isn't it time for me to love you?"

"Probably, but I'm dripping wet. I think I should towel off."

"I have a better idea. Let me lick you dry."

"Licking will only make me wetter," Katherine warned.

"Don't care." Marlena fitted the action to her words.

Thus engrossed, they did not hear the whispering or the laughter that seemed to come from everywhere. It was louder, as if the whisperers were enjoying the activity of the two women in Katherine's bedroom. When the laughter died, the sounds became similar to those being made by Marlena and Katherine — soft cries and groans of pleasure, the wetness of flesh against flesh. None of this would have been clear enough to record, being more an impression of an actual sound, as if the eavesdropper were several rooms away, listening through closed doors.

"I didn't hear anything last night," Katherine said through foam. She was brushing her teeth, standing naked in the bathroom, her back to Marlena who was naked on the bed.

"Neither did I, but I wasn't listening." Marlena sat on the side of the bed. "I didn't think I could ever spend the night in this place again, much less spend it making love with a redhead."

"Too many bad memories? I can understand that."

"When I saw Eva in this very bed with that tramp, I wanted to die. Now, I don't give a damn, thanks to you." Marlena stood and stretched. "I'd better go downstairs. I don't have any clean stuff here." She began gathering clothes from the floor where Katherine had dropped them. "Would you like to go out for breakfast? I have an appointment with a bride and groom at eleven, but that gives us plenty of time."

"Sure, I'd like that. I'll come down when I get dressed, OK?"

Marlena, with an armful of clothes, said, "I have a great idea, Katherine. Why don't you move downstairs with me, and then we won't have to keep walking back and forth so much."

Katherine stood very still. Frowning, she said, "I want to be with you, but I don't know about moving. Isn't that kind of sudden?"

"Katherine Duncan, I'm falling in love with you. Yes, it's sudden, and I've probably scared you to death, but I know I want you, now and forever, if you'll have me."

Katherine burst into tears.

Marlena dropped the clothes and took Katherine in her arms. "I've come on too strong, haven't I?"

Katherine, sobbing quietly, looked up into Marlena's green eyes. "I'm confused. What if I wake up one day and decide I'm not a lesbian?"

"After last night I would take bets. There are some women who like to try it with a lesbian just to say they have. I don't think that's the case with you. But, my darling, I'll take my chances." She smoothed Katherine's hair and kissed Katherine's soft lips. "Now, you'd better dress before that offer of breakfast expires."

The phone rang. Katherine made no move to answer it. Marlena paused for a minute, her eyebrows raised in question. She started down the stairs.

Home after breakfast, Katherine cleaned the

kitchen mess and made the bed. As she changed sheets, she relived moments of their passionate lovemaking. Lesbian love soils sheets, too, she found.

She kept looking at her watch. Marlena had said she'd be back around one o'clock, and the time couldn't fly fast enough for Katherine. The flowers from last night were still fresh, so Katherine put them on the coffee table. Then she sat and waited.

"Are we going to eat at your private club again?" she asked as Marlena whisked the car across the tracks on Canal Street.

"Do you want to?"

"I want what you want," Katherine said primly. "If you're insatiable, I can be too, you know."

Marlena smiled grimly, her eyes on the road. "I'm sorry I frightened you this morning. It wasn't fair to ask you to move in with me, and I know that. It was too soon. You aren't even settled, and I'm pushing you to make changes you might not want. You see" — she reached for Katherine's hand — "I've been the way I am all of my life. I know the kind of person I need to make me happy. You probably have plans that don't include a woman."

Katherine felt tears begin. "Please don't apologize. I'm not frightened of you; I'm scared of myself because I don't know me anymore. You're the first woman I . . . I've ever touched that way, and I'm terrified because I need to do that to you again."

"You need?"

"I've thought of nothing else all morning."

Katherine sniffed. "I never wanted Pam that way. I hardly touched her at all."

Marlena drove without speaking for several blocks. Finally she cleared her throat. "I think we'd better cool it for a while, my love, until you get yourself straightened out. Loving a woman is very natural for me, but I can see the problem you're having. Let's back up and start again from the beginning. We'll take our time getting acquainted and become good friends before dealing with deeper, more permanent issues. Now, let's go back to town and have lunch at the NOLA Hotel buffet."

"I"ve hurt you, haven't I?"

"I don't know that *hurt* is the right term. I feel a little flat. *Disappointed* might be a better description. I got carried away and left out some of the more important considerations. This is a better plan."

Both became quiet, thinking their own thoughts, while Marlena made a U-turn and headed for town, her eyes straight ahead, her hands clenched on the steering wheel.

Marlena let Katherine out at the curb and roared away. This, however, was Marlena's normal takeoff.

As Katherine crossed the veranda, she noticed a white envelope in her mailbox. It was a letter from Archie with two snapshots enclosed, each showing the baby herons in their nest.

In one, the babies were nested together, eyes closed, feet hidden by their downy bodies. In the other they were staring directly at the camera, tiny featherless wings outstretched, mouths gaping. The parent was not in the picture, but Katherine knew that food was just seconds away. She laughed at the eagerness with which the babies awaited the cricket or lizard or fish to be regurgitated into their bottomless stomachs.

I'm so glad the Corps opened those levees upriver, Katherine thought. *They saved you two from certain death. You'll live, and you'll never even know I cared about you.* This thought was so poignant that Katherine burst into tears again.

Chapter 9

"Katherine, we're setting up book signings for next month, first in Alexandria, then in Lafayette, then in Baton Rouge and New Orleans. There'll be a lot of advance publicity around the state. We have two bookstore chains interested, but we'll deal with them after the signings I mentioned."

"I didn't realize we were that close."

"You were put on the front burner, Katherine, which explains the early publication. Because of the university involvement and the fact that you're already well known, we think sales will be phenomenal. I'm excited myself, and I've been involved since the beginning."

"That's very good news," Katherine said.

"We think the story of your year in the swamp would make interesting reading also. Be thinking about that, will you? Have you learned the fate of your baby herons?"

Katherine sighed. She was accustomed to Dr. Beale's rapid delivery, how the good Doctor changed subjects almost in mid-sentence, but nothing Katherine was hearing seemed to sink in this time. *I should be taking notes*, she thought, *or recording, or something, because I won't remember a word of what she's saying*.

"Katherine? Are you there?"

"Uh, yes, I'm here. I was just thinking about the birds."

"Do you know what became of them? Were they washed away?"

"No, I heard from my friend a week ago. As a matter of fact, she sent pictures, and the babies are fine. The Corps opened a levee or two upriver just in time and stopped the river from rising more and flooding the nest."

"Good to hear that. We'll need some publicity pictures. Is there anyone here you'd prefer?"

Prefer to do what? Katherine thought. "I already have photos, Dr. Beale. I'll bring them this week."

"Fine. We'll talk later." The line went dead.

"I'm glad you're excited, ma'am," Katherine said aloud, "but right now, I don't give a damn." She was sitting in her office, staring out the window at nothing. *I don't want to sign books*, she thought. *I can't smile at strangers. I simply don't have the strength.*

Marlena called each morning, her voice friendly, but their brief conversations contained nothing personal. *Why am I being so stupid*, Katherine wondered, *when this perfectly wonderful woman wants to be a part of my life. I enjoy being with her, and making love to her stirred the strongest feelings I've ever experienced. Why can't I throw myself into her arms and live happily ever after? What in hell is wrong with me?*

Several nights, in the wee, quiet hours, Katherine had heard the huge front door slam shut. *Was Marlena coming home from a night at the club?* Katherine wondered. *Did she bang the door, hoping I would hear? Well, I did hear because most nights I haven't done much sleeping. And,* Katherine grumbled, *that's because I stay awake imagining Marlena and whoever in that damn bedroom. I should get a life*, she told herself.

Archie wrote:

Katherine,

I'm returning the pictures you sent. I don't recognize the man, and neither does Danny nor any of his friends. We wonder what the bags are that he's standing behind. They're plastic and full of something, but we don't have a clue. Why don't you come up some weekend? I'd really like to see you.

Katherine examined the pictures again, this time squinting at the bags, or whatever they were. She didn't have a clue, either. *Maybe I will drive over,* she thought. *It will take only an hour. I can take a look at the babies, and eat some of Archie's good cooking. I've been surviving on nothing but toast and canned soup for too long.*

I wonder if Marlena will even notice that my car is gone, she wondered, as she headed across the lake the next morning. The fresh air on the causeway seemed to clear some of the fuzziness from her brain, and she began to enjoy the clear, sunny day.

Archie was waiting. "First thing," she said, "is for me to take you to the rookery. We have plenty of time before supper, and I know you'd like to see those starving-to-death babies."

Alarmed, Katherine asked, "Did something happen to the parents?"

Archie laughed, "Gracious no! But their wings are almost worn to nubs trying to keep those kids full. I've never seen anything alive eat so much! A couple of times I've parked next to the nest just to see them eat. You're going to get a kick out of watching."

Going downriver, Katherine noticed sandbanks that hadn't been there before and a few trees that had fallen over into the water when the banks were undercut by the flood. The hidden entrance to the rookery was the same, and they floated through without trouble. Some of the familiar landmarks were in place, but others had stayed submerged when the water receded or had been swept away.

Archie paddled for a while, and then they glided silently into a natural anchorage between cypress knees where they were concealed, but the nest was in plain view. The babies, now showing scruffy pinfeathers, were awake and active.

After eating, they usually settled quietly, awaiting the arrival of the next meal. As Katherine and Archie watched, both jerked into action, bills agape and wing stubs flapping. They danced frantically as one of the parents lit on the pile of sticks that made up the nest. One baby, slightly larger, got there first. Whatever the parent brought, it was gobbled immediately, and, as if it hadn't eaten at all, the greedy chick began its begging dance again.

Katherine had to cover her mouth to stifle laughter. "I see what you mean, Archie. It's a wonder that baby doesn't pop."

They watched for an hour, sitting quietly in the battered canoe. "Wish I had my camera," Katherine whispered. "I could have shot a whole roll of this feeding frenzy."

"Why didn't you bring it?"

"No reason," Katherine said. *There was a reason, a good reason*, she thought. *My mind is so full of Marlena, I'm not able to think clearly. This has got to stop. I'm going to call her when I get home.*

As Archie backed the canoe, she said, "Want to go over where that man was, the one in your pictures?"

"Sure, why not?"

They didn't find anything. The flooding waters had washed away whatever there was to find.

At the supper table, Archie brought Katherine up to date. "Things stay pretty much the same except, after you left, we did have some excitement. Some kid found a syringe on one of the new sandbars and jabbed his little sister. They took her to the hospital. We heard that she's OK, but when the river patrol started looking around, they found syringes floating all over the place. Found other things, too. Medical type things, they say."

"Could it be from big kids having a party on the river?"

"No, they're empty vials of all kinds of drugs, and syringes from the size diabetics use to needles as big as a garden hose. There's a lot of it, too. More than what a few people could use at a party, even a gigantic party."

"Have you found anything around here?"

"No, Bill Tangy told me they only began finding things down river, a little ways past the rookery. Almost every place they looked where sandbars or fallen trees had made a kind of dam, they found things, even bandages and plastic tubing."

"I wonder why?" Katherine mused. "This is the first time, isn't it?"

"Never happened before that I know of. They've found a couple of bodies over the last ten years, but nothing like the mountain of junk they're finding now." Archie poured more tea. "They have to wear gloves when they handle whatever they pick up. Some stuff is showing up in the lake, too."

Katherine shook her head. "Somebody must have dumped it, I wonder who?"

"*Why* is a better question. Bill says it's all from a hospital, but around here the hospital incinerates their waste, something around two thousand pounds a day, Bill told me. Soon, they're going to convert to another system that's supposed to be more efficient and has something to do with steam. Bill says it's going to be more friendly to the environment, whatever that means."

"Probably means that steam isn't as bad as smoke, I guess."

Archie pushed back her chair. "Let's sit on the dock. I like to watch the river in the evening."

They carried tea and lawn chairs to the landing, and Katherine breathed deeply, enjoying the river smell. "I've missed all this," she said.

They sat without speaking, watching the splash when small fish jumped to escape big fish. Occasionally, there'd be a big splash. "Gar," explained Archie knowingly.

Except for the splashes, the river was quiet. As the light faded, fireflies began their signaling dance. "We used to catch them," Archie pointed out. "We'd fill a jar and pretend we had lightbulbs. I don't think kids do that anymore."

"Probably not," Katherine said musingly, her thoughts back across the lake and the conversation with Marlena.

Headlights in the parking lot interrupted their quiet evening. "Who the hell?" Archie said, rising. She walked toward the lights, and Katherine heard her call out, "Hi, Bill."

Moments later, Katherine heard footsteps on the wooden walkway. Looking over her shoulder, she saw Archie and a very tall man. "Katherine," Archie called, "this is my friend Bill Tangy. Remember, I told you about him?"

Bill sat on the edge of the dock, his feet hanging over, almost touching the water. He smiled at Katherine but didn't offer his hand. "I've heard plenty about you," he said, "and all of it's good. Archie's a big fan of yours."

Katherine smiled, somewhat irritated because he had interrupted her quiet evening. "That's good to hear. I'm one of Archie's fans, too." *Go away and leave us alone*, she thought.

Bill cleared his throat. "Archie said that you'd taken some pictures of a fellow in the swamp, on the outskirts of the rookery. I'd like to take a look at them, if it's OK with you."

"It's fine with me, but I don't have them here."

"Think you could mail them over?" he asked.

"Sure," Katherine said, shrugging. "I'm going back to New Orleans tomorrow. I'll put them in the mail right away." She thought for a moment. "Why do you want to see them?"

"I guess Archie told you about the medical waste we've been finding in the river. Well, I've learned the hospital has farmed out their waste for the last couple of weeks, while the replacement system is being built. Everything was supposed to go to a special landfill, but none of it has shown up there. I think you may have a photo of the waste being dumped in the swamp, and a clear picture of the man doing it."

Katherine sat up straighter. "You really think so?"

She couldn't see Bill's face clearly, but the brim of his hat was bobbing up and down. "Yes, ma'am, I do," he said solemnly.

"Give me your address or your card, and I'll take care of it as soon as I get home."

"Appreciate that." He pushed himself up, and with a nod to both women he walked back to the parking lot.

Neither Katherine nor Archie spoke until his car turned into the dirt road that led to the highway. "Well, Katherine, you might have caught a crook."

"I might at that," Katherine said.

Driving home the next afternoon, with two casserole dishes filled to the brim on the seat beside her, Katherine was pleased that she had enlarged and clarified the photos. *I'm going to love telling Marlena all about this. She'll get a kick, I know.*

One bowl was hot, the other cold, so Katherine put the warm bowl on top and, her arms now full, started climbing up to her kitchen door. She had only taken a step or two when she saw Pam sitting on the landing. Too late to turn around, she continued, thinking that she could use the heavy glass casserole bowls as weapons if it came to that.

"I don't see your girlfriend's car. Has she left you?" Pam had been drinking, Katherine could tell.

Katherine stopped a step below the landing. "You were told not to come back, Pam. So go away." Katherine could feel her pulse beginning to pound out of fear for what Pam could do.

"I don't think so." Pam reached for the bowls, yanking them out of Katherine's arms. "Open the door, bitch, or I'll brain you with these."

Katherine opened the door, and Pam waited for Katherine to go first. Katherine walked to the other side of the kitchen table as Pam kicked the door shut. She clanked the bowls on the table, grinning across at Katherine. "I've had my eyes on you, and I haven't seen your girlfriend around lately. Means you're not getting any, doesn't it?" She began moving around the table toward Katherine.

"Why are you doing this? I haven't done anything to you." Katherine edged away. "Pam, please leave me alone. Anything there was between us is over."

"You ran out on me, and nobody does that." Pam was making little feints with her hands as Katherine moved to keep the same distance between them.

Pam lunged and caught Katherine's blouse, ripping it down the front. Katherine tried to twist away, but Pam held tight. They were still on opposite sides of the table, neither giving ground, when the kitchen doorbell rang. Pam was facing the half-glass door and, with a curse, she let go of Katherine's blouse.

Katherine turned to see a policeman peering at them through the glass. He rang again. Katherine pulled the front of her blouse together, walked around Pam, opened the door, and said, "My friend here is just leaving. Will you let her pass, please?"

No one spoke as Pam turned and stomped out the door and down the stairs. "Did I come at a bad time?" the patrolman asked.

"You probably saved my life." Katherine could feel her face turning red. "We were arguing," she said lamely.

"Well, I'm here to pick up some pictures from you, if you're Katherine Duncan. We got a call from across the lake, and I'm supposed to get them from you and deliver them to the causeway patrol, where a car will be waiting. Myself, I'd send a fax."

Katherine was relieved, and her hands kept shaking long after the young officer had gone. She called Archie.

"Honey, Bill was real excited about those pictures. He said he couldn't wait, so I gave him your address. I hope you don't mind."

Chapter 10

Katherine sat at the kitchen table, elbows resting on either side of her coffee cup. The young policeman had taken the photos, and Katherine felt her fear returning with each step as he clomped down the stairs. Pam could very well be waiting for him to drive away before she tried again.

If I keep thwarting her, she may do something really harmful. I wouldn't be surprised at anything she tried to do to me. If only I knew what she wanted.

With a sigh, Katherine pushed her cup aside. *I'm*

going to look through my portfolio for something of me that looks OK enough for publicity, and then I'll dress and deliver it to Dr. Beale. It's still early enough for her to be in her office. Katherine leafed through an expanding file that contained posed, color photos taken several years ago. She had to smile because at that time her hair had been short, curling over her ears. *I do look a lot younger*, she thought, *but then I was younger.*

She selected a smiling photo, reasoning that she wouldn't be doing much smiling at the book signing if her life didn't make a dramatic turnaround. If people wanted smiles, they could look at the photograph. She touched her hair, now shoulder length. *All this hair has got to go, too*, she reasoned.

In the bathroom, she whacked off one side, then reached to gather a fistful from the other side. Someone tapping on the kitchen door almost caused a heart attack. "I will not answer," she said to the mirror, her knees about to give way.

"Katherine, it's Marlena. Open the door."

"Oh, God," Katherine said. Scissors still clutched in her hand, she almost ran to the door. The lock was new, designed to keep Pam out, and Katherine fumbled with the key of the unfamiliar mechanism, her eyes not leaving Marlena's face.

She fell into Marlena's waiting arms, the scissors forgotten as she hugged with all her strength.

"Whoa, love, watch out for your weapon. It's poking me in the back." Marlena eased away from Katherine's embrace. She held Katherine at arm's length. "Let's move to the living room. We're way too obvious standing here in the door."

Before they sat, Katherine reached for Marlena

again. "I love you," she said in a rush. "I didn't know I loved you until just this minute. I've been stupid and stubborn, and I know this is awfully sudden, but there it is."

"Ah," Marlena breathed. Her kiss was soft and tender, and Katherine returned the kiss with equal gentleness. Their breath mingling, Katherine began fumbling with Marlena's blouse, her hands cupping Marlena's breasts, her body swaying into Marlena's. "I know I'm a lesbian because all I can think of is getting you naked," she said.

"Wait," Marlena said softly as she caught Katherine's hands. "I have to tell you something first."

Reluctantly, Katherine let Marlena guide her to the sofa. "What can be more important than what I want to do to you right now?" Katherine was surprised. "Don't you think we can talk later?"

"Of course. We'll have a lifetime to talk. We'll also have a lifetime to cater to your carnal needs." Marlena was smiling, her eyes on Katherine's very irregular hairline. "I'm afraid to ask what you've done to your hair."

Katherine reached up. "Oh, God," she said, "my hair!"

"Does your hair have anything to do with these?" Marlena held up the scissors.

Katherine laughed aloud. "Bet I really look great. Here, give me those." She took the scissors from Marlena's hand, and placed them on the coffee table. "I'll do something about my hair later. Now, tell me what's so important that I have to hear it before we can jump in bed."

"Earlier, I saw Pam park around the corner. She

knew you weren't here because your car was gone. She was up your stairs before I could get out of my car. Then you got here, and a few seconds later a police car pulled up in front of the house. Well, Pam came flying down the stairs to her car, so I waited, watching to see if she'd try the stairs again. When she finally left, I came up."

"You mean I waited to hear that!" Katherine reached for Marlena again.

"Actually, that's just the background. While you were greeting me so effusively, I saw Pam's car stop at the corner again. I wouldn't be surprised if she were looking in your door right now."

Katherine felt her heart jerk at the thought of facing Pam again. Unconsciously, her hand reached for the torn ends of her blouse. "What am I going to do?"

"You don't have to do anything, love. I'm here now." Marlena smiled reassuringly. "Your new lock is break-in proof, even if she smashes the glass. Without a key she can't get in. And I, my dear, am listening."

"Maybe she won't try if she saw your car."

"I parked on the other side of the street, across the neutral ground, just so she wouldn't see me. Let's just sit quietly and wait for what's going to happen."

With one hand on Marlena's thigh and her other hand clenched in her lap, Katherine leaned into Marlena, her breathing unsteady. "This whole thing is so damn sordid," she whispered.

"The woman is obviously sick," Marlena whispered back. "I can't see the two of you together at all." She was shaking her head in wonder when the sound of breaking glass came from the kitchen. Marlena reached to steady Katherine, who had jumped in fright. "Now we make our phone call," she said, reaching for the phone next to the sofa. She punched buttons and spoke quietly to a person on the other end of the line.

Katherine heard her emphasize the word *now!*

"We are two minutes from the station house, and, unless Pam can fly off that landing, she's going to be caught red-handed." Marlena was smiling. "Now do you see why I wanted to wait?"

Katherine nodded. "You are my hero," she said.

They heard Pam trying to open the lock; they heard the shuffling of several feet; they listened while Pam began a sputtering explanation; then they heard footsteps fading down the steps and a knock on the door. Marlena motioned for Katherine to stay seated. Katherine heard Marlena talking to someone she called Tim. Then Marlena returned to the living room.

"What will happen now?" Katherine asked as they entered the bedroom hand in hand. "What will they do?"

"If you're really interested, I'll find out in the morning. In the meantime, we are free from interruption for as long as we like."

They turned to each other's arms at the same moment. Marlena finally leaned away, saying, "I hope you intend to do something about your hair. I think it should be committed."

"Scissors are on the table in the living room. You may get them if you're in such a hurry, and I'll do some trimming."

"Think I'll wait," Marlena whispered.

* * * * *

"Well," Katherine said, "I like breakfast in bed. You are full of surprises, I didn't even hear you get up."

"Sit a little higher so I can put this tray on your lap without spilling everything," Marlena said.

They sat side by side, propped against the headboard, drinking coffee and sharing buttered toast. "Will I get this every morning?" Katherine asked.

"If you're good."

"Define *good*, please." Careful of the tray, Katherine turned to Marlena. "I can't remember being this happy."

"Honeymoons are supposed to make you happy, my love."

"Is that what we're having? A honeymoon? The thought never occurred to me." Katherine paused, her expression thoughtful. "I like being with you even when we're not having sex."

"When was that?" Marlena laughed aloud. "I remember being seduced by you the second time we ate together. Of course, I was an easy mark because you turned me on just by being you. I think it had something to do with your hair." Marlena eyed Katherine's hair, half long, half short. "If we can ever get out of bed, I'm going to introduce you to my hairdresser. He's pretty good, I think, but whether or not he can repair what you've done . . ."

Katherine said, "I have to cut this long hair first so I won't look so funny just walking in the door." She moved the tray to the bedside table, threw back the sheet, and stalked out of the bedroom.

When she returned, her hair was just below her ears in the front and strung in longer tendrils in the back. Marlena could only stare and shake her head. "Better keep your day job, love, because you'll never make it as a barber." She held out her arms. "Come here."

"Are we going to honeymoon again?"

"If you'll get back in bed we just may do that."

Katherine, now resting full length on Marlena's warm body, said, "I heard them last night."

"I didn't, but you make noise. I can't hear myself think."

"What you do to me requires thought? I heard that lesbian love was spontaneous. I didn't know we needed to think. Next you'll tell me lesbians have a manual."

"Get smart if you like, but there's no future in it. I see there's a lot you have yet to learn." Marlena shifted from under Katherine's body. "Did you really hear them?"

"Yes. I heard laughter, too." Katherine rolled to her back.

"They were laughing?"

"I thought so."

"You bathe first while I clean the mess I made of the kitchen, and then I'll bathe so we can go have a real breakfast." Marlena paused in the bedroom doorway, the tray in her hands. "What are we hearing, Katherine? Is it all in our imaginations?"

"I certainly hope not. Two people don't hear what's not there at the same time." Katherine paused in the bathroom doorway. "What I hear is real; I don't imagine it."

At breakfast they lingered over coffee. They

weren't doing a lot of talking, mostly just gazing at each other across the tiny table. "I don't want to work today, but a carnival krew is having a costume rehearsal of last year's ball so they can show the finery to a group from Atlanta." Marlena shrugged. "They want the same flowers as the original ball, so it's up to me."

"You'll do this by yourself?"

"Heavens no. Four of my people will be there to help. We have to get things set up before noon, in time for the processionals, and get the stuff out of the hotel before the ballroom is put to use for something else tonight. It's going to be a squeeze."

"I'd like to help."

Marlena stood. "I hoped you'd say that. It's not good for couples to separate the first day of their honeymoon. We'll be busy, but you'll get to see the court costumes up close, and we'll be together all day." Marlena took Katherine's elbow and led her to the door, saying in an undertone, "We'll have supper at the club tonight."

When the last of the flowers had been packed in Marlena's huge delivery truck, Katherine heaved a sigh of relief. "I didn't think we'd make it." Hotel personnel were hauling in dining tables as Marlena and her people were wheeling out flowers.

"Are you going to throw those away?" Katherine asked as the truck backed away from the hotel loading dock. "There wasn't anything wrong with them that I could see."

"No, they'll be reassembled as bouquets and

corsages for the ladies of the court and centerpieces for the various wives. The rest will go to a couple of churches. The krew owns them, so I'll get paid again for rearranging and redelivering."

"I certainly hope so. That is a lot of work."

"It's a living," Marlena said, backing her convertible into traffic. "Now, my love, we're headed for some good food, a little dancing if you like, and something else I know you'll like."

"Are you talking about honeymoon again?"

"Yes, I intend to make the most of it while I'm still young."

" 'S OK with me." Katherine laughed.

This time, Katherine saw, there were many women eating, several couples dancing, and a young woman playing a guitar and singing something about love regained or love lost, Katherine couldn't be sure.

The menu wasn't extensive, only four entrées, but they were prepared with goodies Katherine had never heard of. "Maybe if I spoke Swahili I'd know what to eat," she whispered to Marlena.

"Get the steak," Marlena urged, "and salad with house dressing."

It was delicious. Katherine cleaned her plate. "Excellent," she said. "Everything was as good as you promised. Now do we go upstairs?"

"Would you like to dance?" Marlena pointed to the dance floor. "There's room."

"Do I have to dance for my supper? You didn't say anything about that when you lured me here."

Marlena, laughing, motioned for the waitress. "Is there a room?" she asked.

The waitress nodded, eyeing Katherine. "I just checked, Marlena, and ten is ready."

"OK, thanks." Marlena led Katherine up the stairs. Katherine didn't see numbers on the doors, but Marlena stopped at the third door on the left side of the hall. Katherine heard the lock click as Marlena closed the door behind them.

"We've been working all day. Would you like to bathe before we honeymoon?" Marlena was already unzipping her slacks.

"Yes, and I need to brush my teeth, too."

A drawer in the bathroom contained toothbrushes, toothpaste, dental dams, condoms, two kinds of lubricating jelly, bath powder, and a few other things Katherine didn't recognize. Marlena handed Katherine a red toothbrush and took a green one for herself. They brushed and then stepped into the hot tub. Katherine put her toothbrush on a shelf next to Marlena's green one, and entered the tub.

The water was warm and soothing. Katherine let herself float across Marlena's legs. "I've heard it's not a good thing to fuck in a hot tub, but that's what I want to do." She slipped one hand up between Marlena's legs and at the same time began smoothing Marlena's breast with slow tongue strokes.

Katherine snugged her free arm around Marlena's waist so Marlena couldn't float away, and with her fingers she began delicately touching the velvet softness between Marlena's legs.

The water's soothing warmth and the gentle support it gave their bodies made Katherine's movements dreamlike. Her eyes closed, she stroked slowly, fingers easing into Marlena, teeth nibbling at Marlena's breast.

Their involvement was so complete that neither noticed they were slipping off the molded seat and into deeper water. Marlena sank first, Katherine a second later. Whooping and sputtering, they sat up, looked at each other, and screamed with laughter.

"I swallowed half the damn tub," Marlena gasped. "You certainly picked the right moment to drown me." Hair and body dripping, she stood and offered her hand to Katherine. "This is certainly a moment to remember."

"I"ll bet we're not the first," Katherine said, stepping out of the tub and reaching for a towel. "I'm glad my hair is short; it'll dry faster."

"I'm going to tell people we almost drowned making love in a hot tub."

"I'd rather you didn't," Katherine said, "but next time let's be safe and hire a lifeguard."

"Yeah, one with blinders and earplugs."

Chapter 11

"Marlena, do you have to pay for this room? Like a motel, maybe?" Katherine was trying to tame her hair, which had dried as they were tumbling on the bed the night before and looked like the yard full of weeds, as Marlena claimed.

Marlena was putting on her watch. She was dressed except for shoes. She took the brush from Katherine and began combing through the short curls that refused to stay in place. "What has happened here?" she asked. "Yesterday your hair was long and straight; today it's worse than Shirley Temple ringlets." She brushed some more. "No, Katherine, I do not have to pay for our night in this motel. I pay yearly membership dues, and I pay separately for meals and drinks."

"Another thing, I didn't notice numbers on the doors, but you led me straight into this particular room, which I assume is number ten."

"That's right. Will it surprise you to know I'm familiar with each and every room in the house? And, before you ask, yes I have, ah, used them all at one time or another. Remember, I told you I didn't feel right about cavorting in the museum where I live? Well, this place is safe for quickies or for all-nighters or whatever."

Katherine smiled at their images in the mirror. "Define *whatever*, will you?"

Leaning to touch her lips to the back of Katherine's neck, Marlena said, "I loved your long hair, but short hair doesn't get in the way of kisses, or haven't you noticed?"

Katherine took the brush from Marlena's hand. "There's nothing more we can do about this mess. Let's go eat."

They stopped at a waffle place on Canal Street. "Yes, I noticed," Katherine said.

"Noticed what?"

"Kisses and necks," Katherine said, smiling. "I noticed kisses and necks."

"You are remarkable," Marlena announced after the waitress served their coffee. "You are also wonderful and exciting, and if I didn't have three appointments this afternoon we'd spend the day doing *whatever*. After my hairdresser does things with your hair, that is."

"I know I look like a waif, but do you have to keep reminding me?" Katherine pretended hurt feelings.

"You look less like a waif than any waif I've ever seen, my love. And if you gobble your way through that pile of pancakes, you will look like a waif balloon."

"Insult me," Katherine said, pouring maple syrup. "I'm not even listening."

Marlena's hairdresser greeted Marlena with a gushing demonstration of hand waving, and exclamations of delight. "Where have you been, you bad person?" he asked. At the same time, his eyes opened their widest at the sight of Katherine's hair.

"Carlos, my friend needs help," Marlena explained. "We don't have an appointment." She shrugged. "I don't have much time, either."

"My dear, my dear," he gushed, turning Katherine toward an empty chair and the mirror that stretched the length of the room. With a flourish that would have done credit to a Broadway production, he covered Katherine's front with a flowered drape. "I always have time for you," he told Marlena, as he turned Katherine's head from side to side.

After many ah's and hm's he began snipping at Katherine's hair. "Are you Marlena's new love?" he asked. "It's about time."

In the mirror, Katherine watched her face turn beet red. She also saw Marlena's reflection and the laugh Marlena tried to conceal.

"This woman's hair is the most gorgeous color

I've ever seen! Why doesn't she wear it long? It's her crowning glory, you know." He snipped some more. "I know two dozen women who would simply die for natural hair like this."

He began turning Katherine's chair, his expert scrutiny at last satisfied. "There," he said, "I've done the best I could. She looks like a teenaged boy with all those short curls. I could go for her myself."

"Don't get any ideas, Carlos. I don't intend to share." Marlena handed Carlos cash and didn't seem to expect change.

Outside the shop, Katherine said, "I'm almost bald!"

"Nonsense, you look perfectly lovely. In fact, I'm completely turned on, and I think it's the way those curls tease your ears." Marlena reached, her fingers delicately stroking Katherine's neck and ear. "Ummm," she mused, "it's too bad I have those appointments."

"Marlena, what will happen to Pam?"

"When I get to the shop I'll call Tim and explain it was all a mistake and that no charges will be filed. They'll release her, and she'll be on her way, little the worse for wear." Marlena paused. "Maybe she's learned a lesson."

"I hope so. She really frightens me, Marlena. I'm afraid she'll burn down your house to get revenge."

"I suppose there's that possibility, love, but we can't live in fear for the rest of our lives."

"You didn't know you were taking on my troubles, did you?"

"Katherine, I fell for you like a lead balloon. I wanted you from the first moment, before we'd even said hello. I don't know why; it just happened. So if you have troubles, they're now my troubles, too." Marlena was as serious as Katherine had ever seen her.

"I'm sorry I gave you a hard time. It wasn't you I was afraid of; it was me." Katherine sighed. "I didn't want to hurt you then, and I don't want my problems to cause you hurt now. I doubted my own sexuality, you know, and that caused you pain. I don't want you to be hurt again because of me."

"Say" — Marlena turned Katherine's head so they were face to face — "that's enough, love. We're on our honeymoon. Don't give me any lip. Anyway, I have something for you that I was saving for tonight. Will my baby feel better if I give it to her now?" Marlena opened her purse and handed Katherine a small velvet box. "This is because I love you."

The ring was set with diamonds all the way around. "I didn't want anything too ostentatious," Marlena explained, "Just something to act as a reminder when I'm not with you . . . like the rest of this afternoon, as a matter of fact." Marlena looked at her watch. "I have to take you home now, but I'll be back around five."

Katherine, stunned, hadn't spoken. She slipped the ring on her third finger, left hand, then held her hand up for Marlena to see. "If you weren't driving I'd show you how much this means to me. I love it, and I love you."

Katherine put her hand on Marlena's thigh, the diamonds sparkling. "Let's keep it that way," Marlena said, swerving into the driveway. "I'd go up with you, if I could, but I'm already late."

Katherine stood on the curb, watching, as Marlena roared away. She looked at her hand and at the ring glittering in sunlight. *Marlena really loves me,* she thought, *and I love her. I was stupid to be so damn afraid.*

Another bath, a change of clothes, and Katherine began waiting for Marlena. Minutes seemed to drag like hours. She selected one of the lesbian books from the wall shelves, one with a cover picture of two women kissing. The sex began with the first paragraph. Two chapters into the book, the women were still in bed. Katherine giggled aloud. *If I had read this a month ago, I wouldn't have believed a word, but now I know the feeling.*

When, in the third chapter, the protagonist and her girlfriend went on a picnic, Katherine knew why they went and what they were going to do. The picnic was merely to offer a change of scene, their bedroom having spontaneously combusted at the end of chapter two.

I'll have to show this to Marlena if she hasn't read it already. I didn't believe any two people could have sex morning, noon, and night and still not be satisfied. But Marlena and I have been going at it like we were starving, and I'm having a hard time waiting for her to get home. Katherine nodded to herself. *Thinking about Marlena arouses me, and I want to be naked in bed, making love.*

An idea slowly formed. At twenty minutes to five, Katherine put the book away. She went into the bedroom, got undressed, and climbed under the sheet. She lay smiling until another idea formed. "Ah, yes," she said aloud. Smiling more broadly now, she got out of bed, straightened the covers, plumped the pillows, and lay back down. This time she lay on top of the covers.

The next minute she heard the lock turn in the kitchen door. "Katherine," she heard Marlena call.

"Here," Katherine answered.

"I loved your surprise," Marlena called from the bathroom. "Can I expect this every day?"

"Don't be greedy." Katherine was smiling; Marlena could hear it in her tone. "When the book is out, I have to do some signing here and there. I won't be home for days at a time."

"I'll go with you, my dear. I'm the boss, remember? I can get away whenever I like."

Katherine sat up. "Do you mean that?" Marlena walked over to the bed and kissed Katherine's forehead. "Yes, baby, I mean that."

"It's boring, but I have to do it."

"Well, it won't be boring all the time. We can shop and sightsee. Just being with you will be fun for me."

Katherine stood, saying, "I've really dreaded those signings, but now they won't seem so bad."

"I didn't think to ask if you'd eaten. Are you hungry?" Marlena looked at her rumpled clothing. "Answer before I go after some clean clothes so I'll know what to get."

"We should have hung your things so they wouldn't be wrinkled." Katherine watched Marlena roll her eyes toward heaven and knew what Marlena was going to say.

"If you wanted me to have unwrinkled clothes, you should have been under the sheet, not on top of it. There was no way I could hang my clothes, not with you writhing naked on the bed. I am not a wooden Indian."

"I wasn't writhing. I was just moving to attract your attention. So, there!" Katherine stalked into the bathroom, Marlena's hearty laughter ringing in her ears.

They didn't go to the club. Marlena thought Katherine would like to have dinner in the famous revolving room at the top of New Orleans's newest hotel. They had wine and ate by candlelight as the restaurant turned slowly above the city lights. "I'd like to know how this thing turns three hundred and sixty degrees without snapping off at the base, but I'm afraid you'd tell me if I asked." Katherine was fascinated by the panoramic view.

"I don't know," Marlena answered. "I've never thought about it."

"Our waiter knew you. Do you come here often?" Katherine nodded her thanks when he poured more wine. "I'm not being nosy, just that I want to know everything you've ever done or said."

In the candlelight, Marlena's green eyes seemed full of stars. She took a sip of wine. "My uptown shop decorates this place every other day. Haven't you noticed the flowers?" Another sip. "I felt it was my duty to make sure everything we send is fresh and colorful, so I eat here fairly often."

Katherine nodded. "There's more to that, isn't there?"

"Ah, yes, there is." Marlena took a deep breath. "Eva liked it here better than any other restaurant, so the two of us were here more often than I liked. I found out later, quite by accident, that Eva's new girlfriend would occasionally sub at night. I was really bringing Eva here so she could ogle the woman's strapless, low-cut neckline. After a while, Eva didn't have to come here, she had the tramp in our bed."

"I had to ask, didn't I?" Katherine grimaced.

" 'S OK, love, I don't really care. I have you, and if Eva had been faithful, you and I wouldn't have met. I think it's fate, don't you?"

"Maybe I can look at Pam as an instrument of fate. I wouldn't be here if it wasn't for her."

Marlena raised her glass. "Let's toast the fate that brought us together."

Their glasses touched. The tiny clink was an affirmation of their love.

Chapter 12

They were awakened by the sound of laughter. They lay, unmoving, listening. Marlena nudged Katherine with her elbow. "I know you're awake. Do you hear them?"

"Yes," Katherine whispered back. "I hear them. Only, who is 'them'? Who are *they*, I mean."

Marlena turned so that her mouth was close to Katherine's ear. "One of them is Aunt Helen. I'd bet money on it."

"Let's don't get into that again. I know your

Aunt Helen is dead. You told me she died last year. I even know where she's buried."

"Katherine, I'm not joking. That's Aunt Helen; I know it is. I recognize her laugh."

"From what you've told me, she didn't do much laughing, so how do you know?"

"Come." Marlena threw back the covers. "Let's go sit in the kitchen and I'll tell you how I know."

With coffee saucered and blown, they sat at the table, both wide awake now. "You see," Marlena began, "Aunt Helen, for sixty some years, thought her lover had deserted her. She carried on, of course, and built three very profitable flower shops."

Marlena sipped the hot liquid. "As far as I know, she was never close with anyone, but she was a pleasant person, and I loved her very much. As a matter of fact, I was named for the woman she loved those many years ago. Well, in the last year of her life she learned that the original Marlena hadn't deserted her at all. Marlena was killed, probably on the way to meet Aunt Helen in Chicago where they intended to begin a life together."

Katherine saw Marlena's eyes brim with tears. "It's such a sad story," Marlena said. "I can't think about it without crying. The happiest moment of Aunt Helen's life during those long, lonely years was the day she learned that her darling Marlena had not stopped loving her, and if not for Marlena's death, they would have spent those sixty years together. That's when I heard Aunt Helen really laugh as if she were finally happy."

Katherine's eyes filled, too. "I feel so sorry for Aunt Helen," she sniffed. Turning her head toward the elevator shaft, Katherine said, "I don't hear them now, do you?"

Marlena sat very still for a moment, listening, but there were no sounds in the quiet apartment. She looked at Katherine, her expression troubled. "What are we hearing, Katherine? It's not an animal, not street noises, not the house settling; it's nothing I can explain. I feel that I should do something, but I don't know what." They stared at each other.

"It really bothers you, doesn't it? I know it bothers me." Katherine ran her hand through her short curls. "Marlena, it's almost beginning to scare me."

Marlena's expression was bleak. She shook her head slowly. "I'm not afraid. I've lived in this place for too many years to let some sounds frighten me, but I am concerned." She reached for Katherine's hand. "Let's go back to bed. I'll hold you."

They did not fall asleep immediately, even though no more sounds kept them awake. Katherine drifted, comforted by the warm embrace of Marlena's arms; Marlena, half dreaming, felt Aunt Helen's gentle touch and heard the softly whispered, "Good night, my child."

Over breakfast, Marlena informed Katherine that she was going to look for a psychic in the phone book. "Whatever it is, it isn't normal, so maybe it's paranormal."

"You don't believe that, do you?" Katherine was more than a little surprised. Marlena was so practical, so realistic. "Are you in the habit of consulting these people?"

"Well, no, I never have. It came to me last night that maybe the house is haunted. Like castles are supposed to be. The place isn't hundreds of years old, but neither is it new." She paused as another idea surfaced. "Say, maybe we ought to have a séance; the ghosts may be trying to communicate with us." Marlena tried to hide her smile.

"I can tell you're joking, but if you think we'll learn where a treasure is buried, I'll go along with it."

That afternoon Marlena called. "Katherine, I've contacted a Madame Verna who will be happy to inspect the house for spirits or whatever, for a fee, of course. She'll be over after dark tonight."

Madame Verna was short, round, and wore silk bedroom slippers. Her dress reached the floor and then some. She had what looked like a tablecloth with fringe around her shoulders, but she was friendly and not in the least mysterious.

"Tell me why you called, please," she said to Marlena. "I need some history and a description of the noises you mentioned when you called."

This threw Marlena somewhat. She explained later to Katherine that telling everything would be like giving Madame Verna answers before the questions had been asked. So Marlena simply said, "We've been hearing noises coming from somewhere in the house. It sounds like two people, and it isn't frightening, just annoying. What we want to know is who's doing it and why."

Madame Verna nodded. "I'll have to enter every room to identify the psychic sources. You may walk with me, but you must not interrupt if I am contacted by a spirit."

Katherine and Marlena agreed to this, and they walked down the inside stairs to the first floor, following on Madame Verna's heels. Madame Verna walked slowly, clutching her shawl, and she moved through all of the downstairs rooms. Her seemingly aimless meandering as she visited some rooms twice, was brought to a halt in the dining room. Marlena thought a spirit was about to come forth or fly over or whatever a spirit did to make contact. Katherine thought Madame Verna was counting the silver service on the table, the platters, and the huge silver coffee urn on the long sideboard. Whatever, Madam Verna swept out of the room and entered the hall again.

Marlena, who had been walking a few steps behind, caught up with Madame Verna and asked, "Well?"

"This floor, with the exception of the sitting room at the end of this hall, is full of the spirits of those long dead. I sense only the presence of four older spirits in the sitting room, but they are making no effort to contact me. We'll go up now."

Madame Verna paused longest in Marlena's bedroom, but she didn't comment on the spirits that were, or weren't, present. At times she breathed heavily, but did not explain. Whether the loud, seemingly uncontrollable, breathing was due to the influence of the spirits or the number of steps she had climbed, was unclear.

They walked more stairs to Katherine's apartment. Madame Verna became agitated. "There is an evil spirit here," she announced. "I can feel a presence." Her voice took on a sepulchral tone. "Yes, there is an evil presence here." Her eyes closed and she plopped on the couch, seemingly exhausted.

"Who's the spirit?" Marlena asked. "What's it want?"

"The spirit didn't make contact tonight. I will have to return and establish rapport, and then I will tell you."

"You mean we have to do this again?" Katherine blurted.

"These things take time, my dear. Yes, I will have to return."

After ushering Madame Verna to the kitchen door, Marlena gave her a check and assured her that they would not need her services again. She closed and locked the door.

"The woman's a fraud," Katherine exclaimed, "an out-and-out crook! She could no more sense spirits than I can. At least I can hear the noise, whether it comes from spirits or bats in the belfry."

"So much for psychic powers." Marlena grinned. "At least it was entertaining."

Dr. Beale did a double take when Katherine walked into her office. "My goodness, you've certainly changed. Why in the world did you cut your hair?" she asked.

"I thought it would be cooler," Katherine answered. "I used to wear it short, and in this publicity photo it's cut about the same length. I'll be recognizable, I hope." Katherine took the photo out of a large envelope and put it on Dr. Beale's desk.

Dr. Beale looked at the photo, looked at Katherine, and smiled. "Yes, it's you," she said.

"Do you have the itinerary for the signings?"

"I do," Dr. Beale replied, nodding. "I have the list here somewhere." She leafed through stacks of papers and found a folder with Katherine's name on it. "This hasn't been finalized, but I think we can assume the dates will remain the same." She handed the folder to Katherine. "Will you be driving alone?"

"No, a friend will be with me." Katherine smiled. *My lover will be with me*, she thought, *and we will honeymoon all over the state. I may not have the strength to sign my name after a day or two.*

"Well, I'm glad you'll have company. You'll sign for two hours, and each store will have the book displayed on a table that's been set up for you. You'll be interviewed, of course, but the interviews will take place during the signings."

"I won't have anything to do with the sale of the book, will I?"

"No, the stores will take care of that. All you have to do is smile and sign your name. Occasionally you'll be asked to write something personal or dedicate the book to someone other than the buyer, but I'm sure you can handle anything asked of you." Dr. Beale was beaming. "We've had advance sales, you know, and the book isn't even out yet. I must say, Katherine, we're very pleased."

Katherine folded her copy of the itinerary. "I'm glad we used the photos I selected for the book. For me, there was something personal about each one. Did you select the title, Dr. Beale?"

"It was selected by a committee of which I am a member. There were many names submitted, of course. We all agreed that *Big Cypress* was appropriate. Only one other person on the committee knew it was the title you submitted."

"How did you know?" Katherine asked.

"Professor Leger is a very good friend of mine. He's chairman of our committee, and he told me about your visit and his conversation with you."

"I see." Katherine remembered Dr. Leger, his cluttered office, and his kindness. She stood. "Thanks for your time, Dr. Beale."

Katherine felt bouncy as she drove back to the apartment. The book was finished, at least her part of it, and she was deeply in love with a woman who returned that love. *Marlena and I were meant to be together*, she reasoned. *Everything in my entire life led me to this time and this place.*

As she entered the kitchen, the phone rang. Marlena was excited. "I've found a real psychic, " she said. "I had one all along but just didn't know it."

"Where do you have a psychic? Are you kidding me?"

"Honest, love, this woman does some arranging for me every once in a while. She always seems to call me just before I decide to call her. When I comment on the coincidence, she says, 'I'm psychic.' I didn't know she meant it." Marlena laughed. "She's a down-to-earth person, very funny, but she feels and sees things other people don't. I asked her to come over tonight, and she agreed."

"What did you tell her, and how much does she charge?"

"I just told her we heard noises, and she doesn't charge. She says it's a gift she's had since childhood. You'll like her, Katherine."

"Is she coming before or after we eat?"

"After. We'll hop over to Magazine Street for po'boys, if that's OK. She'll show up about seven-thirty."

"Fine, my darling. Try to get home a little early so we'll have a minute or two before we go out to eat."

"What if I leave now? That'll give us more than a minute."

"More is better," Katherine said. "I'll be waiting."

Katherine heard Marlena on the stairs, two steps at a time. She had the door open when Marlena reached the landing. They embraced. "What took you so long?" Katherine asked.

Marlena's psychic was a plain woman with a friendly smile, and Katherine liked her immediately. "I'm Peggy," the woman said, offering her hand. "I hope I can help."

"What do you want us to do? That is, if you're ready for us to do anything. We'll follow you," Marlena said, "or stay out of your way, whatever you say."

Peggy shrugged. "I'm not a professional; I just get impressions. Right now" — she frowned. "I'm sensing a great deal of happiness in this room. It's like the tinkling of tiny bells, as if two lovers were together after a long time." She looked at Marlena. "Don't confirm any of these feelings. That tends to confuse me. Just let me stand here." Once or twice Peggy tilted her head to one side, as if listening, but she didn't say anything.

Marlena reached for Katherine's hand. They stood statue still, watching Peggy.

"The happiness feels recent, but underlying it, I sense water and a death and a dark hole in the ground. I hear gunshots, but they're far away. Overwhelmingly, there's sadness building also. I sense time passing, like calendar pages flying away in the wind, and the sadness growing deeper."

Marlena looked at Katherine, her eyes wide. Their hands gripped tighter.

Peggy said, "These are the impressions, the feelings, I have in this room. Beneath all this, I feel rage and a betrayal. Again, the sadness has grown over a great length of time, but the rage is newer." She looked at Marlena. "I'd like to go downstairs, if it's OK."

They stopped on the second-floor landing. Peggy moved down the hall as if she knew the house. She stopped outside Aunt Helen's bedroom door. "Open please," she said to Marlena. Two steps into the room she turned, shoving Marlena and Katherine aside in her haste to get back into the hall.

"The sadness is too thick to bear," she said softly. "Now, down to the first floor, please."

Again, moving as if she had a floor plan, Peggy walked to the sitting room at the end of the long, wide hall. She opened the door and began smiling. "There's a suitcase, letters, clothing . . . and great happiness here."

Katherine felt Marlena's hand clamp like a vise. Marlena's expression was one of wonderment. "Please," she asked, "what else?"

"Like upstairs, I feel love and great happiness. The lovers, whoever they may be, are trying to release years of despair. That's the best way I can put it. If you hear them at times it's because their happiness overflows."

"Could they be trying to tell us something?" Katherine asked.

"I don't know. I've told you my impressions. Sometimes I get very clear pictures; other times, like now, it's a feeling I can't always put into words." Peggy looked apologetic. "I"m not trying to sell you on life after death or spirits contacting the living or anything wacky. I don't know why I feel what I feel. You might be able to make sense of what I've told you because I certainly can't."

Long after Peggy left, Marlena listed what Peggy had said into a sort of outline. They would try to remember each of her impressions, and Marlena would fill in facts from her own knowledge. Everything seemed to fit.

Still excited, but yawning, they went to bed. "Do you believe Aunt Helen and Marlena are here in the house, making up for all those years they were apart?" Katherine asked this seriously.

Marlena didn't answer for several minutes. "I think their spirits are present, and they let us hear their happiness. I don't know if spirits have form, or even what a spirit is, but I loved Aunt Helen, and she loved me. Why not let me know that her long wait is over? I'm glad she's with Marlena. They loved each other like I love you."

"Will we hear them again, do you think?"

"Maybe, we'll have to wait and see."

Chapter 13

"Katherine, would you like to move away from here?"

"No, I'm perfectly happy, except that I wish we were both occupying the same floor. I know you don't want to live up here with all the bad memories, but I can't see myself living downstairs, as beautiful as your house is."

"Well, I meant both of us moving, of course. On the lakefront there's a new high-rise ready for occupancy, and I've talked with the manager and been out there to see it. The place is beautiful. It's the best I've ever seen. We could be very comfortable."

"Sounds like you've already decided."

"I haven't decided, just inquired." Marlena shrugged. "What to do with this house is the problem. I suppose we could rent this upstairs, but the downstairs is a museum, and I don't think it's rentable. We could just leave it and decide later."

"What prompted this decision? I can see you've made up your mind."

"Not really. It has a lot to do with Aunt Helen and Marlena. We haven't heard them for a week, and I think they're gone. I think maybe there's no need for them to hang around anymore, if that's what they were doing."

Katherine looked out the window at the sun and the blue sky and the normalcy of it all. She shifted under the cover, turning on her side so that they were facing. "I listened to what Peggy said, and what she felt, but I do not believe in spirits or ghosts or haunts of any kind. Maybe people do leave impressions of their presence in the air, or on the walls, when they die. Maybe such a thing is possible; I wouldn't know." Katherine's expression was thoughtful.

She paused, then continued earnestly, "I do feel that your Aunt Helen couldn't care what happens to this house, any more than the others who lived here over the years. They're gone, my love, and even the memory of most of them is gone, too. Was the noise we heard Aunt Helen and her lover? I don't think there's an answer to that. All along it was eerie, but I was never really afraid, nor did I ever feel a malevolent presence. Before Peggy came, I was beginning to be a little apprehensive, simply because what we heard was so far outside of my experience."

Marlena interrupted. "It's just that this place has been in our family for so damn long."

"That may be, my darling, but you aren't going to leave any heirs. You said you were the very last of the line. So sell the place if you need money, or give it to some historical society. I'm sure the furnishings alone, in the original rooms and in place for generations, would drive a collector bananas."

"Yes, I've had offers . . . very generous offers," Marlena said. "For years the historical society has wanted it on the annual tour of homes. I always refused."

"Why not start thinking along those lines?"

Stretching, Marlena snuggled deeper under the covers. "I am thinking along a certain line right now, one that involves you."

"Oh?" Katherine let her hand search, finding two soft mounds, then moving lower to feel the silken hair where Marlena's legs parted. Lightly, Katherine's fingers tapped until Marlena moved her thighs apart, allowing Katherine to stroke through the moisture that formed and spread as Katherine moved her fingers.

"I'm going to make love to you, do you mind?" Katherine whispered, moving so that her face was level with Marlena's breasts, the nipples within reach. "Do you like this?" she asked, her tongue licking the soft flesh.

Marlena groaned and turned on her back, legs stretching wide. "I think I'm going to like it very much," she said hoarsely.

"I figured you would," Katherine said.

* * * * *

Marlena was dressed, ready to meet with the captain of a carnival krew about flowers for the auditorium. "Meet me for lunch?" she asked.

"Of course," Katherine said, smiling. "Do you plan to eat at the club?"

"Thought we would," Marlena answered, snapping shut her briefcase. "We're still on our honeymoon, right?"

"I think continuing orgy is a better name for it, my darling."

"But you're interested, aren't you?" Marlena was grinning, her green eyes full of mischief. "I have a surprise you're going to love, but you'll get it after we climb the stairs at the club, not before."

"I have to give you my body in exchange for some unknown something, is that it?" Katherine rolled her eyes, and shook her head. "The things I do for love!"

Both grinning, they embraced, holding the other close. "I have to hurry; it's almost lunch hour now," Katherine said. "I think I'll stay naked to save time."

"Hussy," Marlena whispered into the tender flesh of Katherine's neck. "I haven't recovered from this morning, and you're tempting me again." She let her hands slide down Katherine's back, cupping Katherine's cheeks, drawing Katherine's pelvic area tight against her own.

Katherine moved her hips seductively. "Are you serious?" she whispered. "Your appointment is only twenty minutes from now; I don't think we have time."

"Spoilsport." Marlena straightened her blouse,

tucking the ends back in her slacks. "Don't be late for lunch," she called from the doorway.

Katherine locked the door and went into the bathroom. She soaked for long minutes under a warm spray, her thoughts on Marlena and the frequency of their lovemaking. *If anybody had told me I'd want sex morning, noon, and night, I'd have said they were out of their mind*, Katherine thought, as she lathered her hair. *Being with Pam used to arouse me, but what I feel in Marlena's arms is sheer heaven.* Katherine stepped out of the shower, walked to the wall mirror, and looked at herself.

"You're not too bad," she said aloud. Her red hair, wet, was a deep auburn, but her pubic hair was undeniably red. "You're a two-toned hussy," she told her image.

Finding a parking place within a block of Marlena's Canal Street store was usually an impossibility, but Katherine pulled into a space being vacated by a delivery truck. *Today is my lucky day*, she thought.

In the shop's huge display window, Katherine watched her reflected image cross the sidewalk to the door. It opened as she reached for the handle. "Come in," Marlena said to the tinkling of bells disturbed by the door. "I've been waiting."

Marlena gave Katherine the twenty-five-cent tour, introducing the employees and showing her the walk-in cooler where flowers were stored, the worktables where the flowers were made into whatever design the customer ordered, and the storeroom where supplies were kept. "My office is very small," Marlena said. "You'd have to sit on my lap." Her smile told Katherine that lap sitting wouldn't be such a bad idea, but her shrug indicated the time wasn't right; too many people were wandering around.

In Marlena's convertible, heading for the lake, Katherine asked, "When do I get my surprise?"

"Aha, do you want it now, or after we eat? It's up to you, my dear."

Katherine touched Marlena's thigh. "Do you really want to know what I'd like?"

"Of course I do."

"I am not a patient soul. I want the surprise, and then I want lunch, and then I want to spend the rest of the day upstairs. How does that sound?"

Marlena laughed aloud. "Up to you," she said, swinging the car in a U-turn and heading back in the direction from which they started. They passed Marlena's shop, but several blocks farther up Canal Street, Marlena swerved the car into the curb. "Here we are," she announced, opening her door.

"Here where?" Katherine asked. They were parked in front of a building with a storefront. It was one story, brick, with flower boxes under the single large display window. Katherine got out of the car and joined Marlena on the sidewalk. Curious, she followed Marlena, who produced a key and opened the building's door.

"This is yours," Marlena said, "all yours."

"What do you mean?" Katherine looked around the large empty room, mystified.

"You've been hanging around the apartment with

nothing to do every day except wait for me. I like that, of course, but you need something to do, don't you?" Marlena didn't wait for Katherine's answer. "In Mobile you had a store of your own. Now, in New Orleans, you'll have another store of your own. That's what this is, my dear, a building in a good traffic area where you can build your business again and where I can visit you from time to time during the day."

"Marlena, you've got to be kidding! A diamond ring is one thing, but a building is something else. I can't let you do this."

"It's already done, Katherine. It's a done deal, as they say. I can't have you getting bored with us. We both need activity outside of the bedroom, and I have my shops to keep me fairly busy, but you have nothing now that your book is finished. Please," Marlena implored. "Please do this, Katherine."

Katherine turned to stare out the display window, a faint frown on her forehead. Marlena watched, unmoving, her face anxious as she waited for Katherine to speak.

Finally, Katherine turned, her expression very serious. "I think I'd like to open a studio and shop like the one I had. I've been wondering what to do all day, and publicity from the book would give me a head start if I opened a studio here in New Orleans." She held out her hands to Marlena. "I love your surprise," she said simply, her eyes beginning to brim with tears.

"For goodness sake, don't start crying." Marlena fumbled for a tissue. "I was so scared you'd throw the building at me. We know each other very well in bed, but we aren't that closely acquainted otherwise. I don't know your favorite color, if you like football, or even your birthday."

Marlena led Katherine to the car, her arm around Katherine's waist. "I promise not to interfere with however you want to set this up. I'll help, of course, if you want me to, but you're the boss, understand?"

Katherine laughed. "I'm a waif, but I'm far from broke, Marlena. We'll talk about all this later, when I've had a chance to think."

"You noticed that the room was very long? Think about this for a minute. You could partition the front as a showroom, make yourself a darkroom and a supply room in back of that, and then the rear could be a sort of . . . a place to make coffee, with a table, a fridge, a couch, and your office things." Marlena was outlining rooms with her hands, the steering wheel forgotten for the moment.

Alarmed, Katherine raised her chin in the air, saying, "I will entertain your suggestion, my dear, but I might want to do something entirely different. Remember, I'm the boss. Now, please watch what you're doing."

"Already I was telling you what to do, wasn't I?" Marlena put her hands back on the steering wheel.

"You've had time to think about this; I haven't. Do you want to stop at a hamburger place so we can talk, or do you want a sandwich at your club?"

"What do you think?"

"I opt for a sandwich at the club. We'll have time to talk later."

This time, the young waitress greeted them both by name. "The same?" she asked as she served their tea. At their nod, she turned away, heading for the kitchen. "She's cute," Katherine said, her eyes following the sway of the woman's hips.

"My God, we're planning a life together, and you're already sniffing out a younger woman." Marlena pretended outrage.

"No, I'm not," Katherine protested. "You know I'm not!"

"It's a good thing. Angela's lover is ten feet tall, and about as wide, and she takes offense if you even look at Angela."

"Marlena, that was the first time in my life that I really looked at a woman. Could I be a lesbian, do you think?"

"We'll find out after lunch. I have some ideas on the subject, but they need testing."

"I love being with you," Katherine said. Looking around the half-filled room to make sure she would not be overheard, she half whispered, "I'm ready to go upstairs this minute. Thinking about you and bed has made me very ready."

"We can eat later," Marlena suggested.

"Let's," Katherine replied.

When they came downstairs, Angela met them at the bottom of the stairs. "I saved your lunch," she smirked. "Think you can eat now?"

Katherine resisted saying, "We already have."

Later, Marlena followed Katherine's car home. Marlena pulled into the short driveway; Katherine parked on the street. They walked together to the outside stairs. As Katherine unlocked the door, Marlena said calmly, "Pam is parked around the corner, Katherine." Katherine's shoulders stiffened; she started to turn. "No, don't look," Marlena hissed.

Inside the kitchen, Katherine faced Marlena. "Can we call the police? That's the only thing that'll deter her."

"No, she hasn't done anything. She's parked legally, and there's nothing you can do."

"When will it end?" Katherine slowly shook her head. She took a deep breath. "When you said you'd visit the place on Canal Street from time to time, I remembered how Pam would drop by the place in Mobile when she felt like it, and we'd fall on the couch, tearing at each other. Sex was more of a confrontation than an act of love." Tears began.

"Please don't cry, my darling." Marlena produced a tissue. "Dry your eyes now, and you can tell me what you've planned for your store. Do you have a name?"

Katherine had to laugh. "When have I had time to think of a name? Between satisfying you in bed, and choking down that dried-out sandwich, I haven't even had my mind in gear."

"Well, let's go sit and try to keep our hands to ourselves. I love to draw plans. You tell me what you want, and I'll sketch it for you."

"Yes, boss," Katherine hooted. "I'd love a hot tub; think you can work that in?"

Chapter 14

For Katherine the days seemed to fly. Each morning she was out of the apartment early, finding great satisfaction in unlocking the door of her soon-to-be studio and photo store. "Why shouldn't I sell supplies?" she asked Marlena one evening. "I don't intend to develop film commercially, except for my own shots, and my darkroom will be a perfect one-man operation for anything I need . . . one-woman, I mean." Katherine was making a list, one of a dozen she had made already.

"Is that a list of things for me to do?" Marlena

watched, her eyes widening as Katherine's pen scribbled line after line.

"Not exactly, but I do need the name of your accountant. I think I've managed to wade my way through most of the city requirements for permits and stuff, also things I need for the state." Katherine looked up. "It's very hard to get a straight answer most of the time."

Marlena wrote on a page of the blank notebook in front of her. "Here's his name and phone number. You probably should have talked with him first."

"I meant to," Katherine said.

"When are the painters coming? You know I've called them twice already. I think you should look for somebody else. If they can't start on time, who's to say they'll ever finish according to your schedule?" Marlena was speaking from experience.

"If they don't start in the morning, I'll do just that. I wish people would do what they say they'll do. Why don't they, do you think?"

Marlena started to answer, but Katherine's attention was on her ever-expanding list, her question rhetorical. "Katherine, we've been at this for hours, don't you think we could go to bed now?"

Katherine looked up; her thoughts at that moment were on light fixtures. "What, darling?" she asked.

"Bed, I want to go to bed." Marlena said, pushing her chair away from the table. She stood, holding out her hand.

Katherine stared, a faint frown creasing her forehead. She stood and walked around the table. "I'm neglecting you, aren't I?" She took Marlena's outstretched hand and pressed it to her lips. "You're the one person in this world I love, and I'm neglecting you."

"I'd say that, too." Marlena put her hand on the back of Katherine's neck, slowly pulling Katherine toward her until their lips met. Their kiss was slow and soft. Katherine's arms reached to enfold Marlena in a close embrace. "I'm ashamed," Katherine whispered, her tongue exploring Marlena's lips.

Marlena felt tingles and the first tiny throb between her legs as Katherine's tongue moved into her mouth. When their tongues met, Marlena's pulse strengthened and a warm, wet feeling spread.

"Do you feel what I feel?" she asked Katherine when they parted to breathe.

"I'm not sure," Katherine answered, "but you can find out." She moved her body slightly so that Marlena could reach between her legs.

"These slacks have a zipper," Katherine offered, as Marlena fumbled with the waistband, trying to find an opening. A moment later, zipper undone, her hand slipped under Katherine's briefs, moving down until her fingers crossed the mound of hair and slipped firmly between Katherine's legs and into Katherine's wet, silky opening.

"What was the question?" Marlena asked as Katherine squirmed, bearing down on Marlena's moving fingers.

"Whatever the question, the answer is yes." Katherine lowered her slacks. "Help me, please."

Marlena opened Katherine's blouse. Together, they managed Katherine's bra, briefs, and slacks. Naked, Katherine backed into the table, sliding over the edge until she sat upright, arms around Marlena's neck.

"Reach behind you for the light," Katherine ordered. "Then hand me a chair cushion."

Marlena did as she was told. She helped Katherine lie back on the table. In the dim light, she could see Katherine's smile.

"Have you ever done it on the kitchen table before?" Katherine was snuggled against Marlena. "Our bed is more comfortable, but I can't remember being so aroused. You really turned me on."

"I think you turned yourself on, standing naked in the middle of the kitchen. Is that why you wanted the light out, so people looking in the door couldn't see what we were doing?"

"I realize you can't see too much from street level, but a naked woman with her legs in the air might give someone a clue. I've heard about people having sex in unconventional places, so I guess that's what we did tonight." Katherine moved her leg so that it rested across Marlena's lower body. "I think we both enjoyed our quickie, don't you?"

"Was that a quickie? It didn't feel like one."

Katherine laughed. "You were so turned on by the time we got your clothes off that you came like the minuteman. I think I liked what we did, but it won't take the place of our usual bedtime activity in our usual place."

Marlena raised herself on her elbow. "I certainly hope not," she said. "Now kiss me good night, unless you want the usual again." Her hand pulled Katherine closer. Their lips touched, and Katherine said, "Yes, please, I'll have the usual."

* * * * *

The painters arrived late but prepared to paint. Katherine told the young man who was in charge, "You're getting paid by the job, but I expect a full day's work every day. If you take off for any reason, don't come back. Understand?"

Surprised, he agreed. They finished in two days, did a creditable job, and cleaned up afterward. Katherine was pleased.

"Spend some time with me today, and I don't mean on the couch," she said to Marlena over morning coffee. "The store fixtures will be delivered this noon, if I can believe the office supply manager, and I'm still not sure where I want things placed. I know," she grinned, "I decided all this already, but now I may have changed my mind."

"Would you like to look at the thousands of potential arrangements I sketched for you? One of them surely must be right, don't you think?" Marlena took out her sketch pad and began flipping pages. "See," she said, "why don't you look through here again?"

"It's one thing to look at a drawing, but thin lines on paper don't really give me a feeling of the space available. I need you there to help me push things around. That's the only way I'll be satisfied."

"Don't tell me that, because there are other ways to satisfy you, and I know a few of them." Marlena buttered the last half of her banana muffin. She watched Katherine's expression and admired the silky curls that were reaching below Katherine's ears now. "Your hair grows like weeds. Did you know that?"

"Yes, I know that, and I think I should see Carlos

again soon. Think we can get an appointment?" Katherine didn't wait for a reply. "I also think I should call Archie. It's been weeks."

"I'll call Carlos this morning. Now, are there any other chores before I see you around noon? What about lunch? Do we eat before the furniture or after?"

"You decide, my darling. If you're free all afternoon we can eat after. What I'm going to do this morning is hang blinds in the front room, so I'd better get moving." Katherine gathered an armload of papers and her purse. She kissed Marlena and breezed through the kitchen door and down the steps.

Marlena sipped at the last of her coffee, staring at the kitchen wall, her thoughts wandering. *Katherine is a workaholic*, she said to herself, *and I don't know if I like being in second place. I'd rather she focused on me. Maybe when everything is finished she'll have more time for us, because she certainly doesn't now.* With a sigh, Marlena put dishes and cups in the sink before going out and locking the door behind her.

"Look," Katherine said as Marlena walked through the shop's front door later that morning, "my first piece of mail!" She was holding up a large, white envelope.

"What is it?"

"It's probably one of the permits I need." Katherine tore open the envelope. "That's what it is," she said, waving a square of paper. "They were moving so slowly at City Hall, I didn't think I'd get any of this in my lifetime."

Marlena looked around the room. "You finished the blinds, I see. Looks good."

"Let me show you our cozy back room. It's completely finished now. The office area is separate from our kitchen, dining room, honeymoon-and-whatever room." She took Marlena's hand and led her past the studio, the bathroom, and the darkroom, and into the private room. "This is just for us. You'll be able to park in back and use the back door like you do at the club. As I see it, the only difference is we won't have to climb stairs."

"Where's the Jacuzzi?"

"I knew you'd ask that. My love, next time you feel like an architect, design an add-on room for the back. We'll put the tub there." Katherine reached for Marlena, put her hands on either side of Marlena's face, and whispered, "I know I've been neglecting you since I started this project, but I wanted to have this place ready when we get back from the book signings. We only have a week until I sign in Alexandria, and then I'll be all over the state for the rest of the month." They kissed tenderly, and Katherine's lips were soft on Marlena's. "It would have been very hard for me to go away with all there was to do here. I promise that you'll get all the attention you could possibly want once we're on the road. I love you. You're all I want. Please remember that."

Marlena looked into Katherine's brown eyes; her arms tightened, drawing Katherine closer. "I'll remember that all my life," she promised, her lips touching Katherine's forehead. She touched Katherine's face with tiny kisses until their lips met. Their kisses became longer as tongues explored; their arms tightened as they breathed into each other. Marlena had Katherine's blouse unbuttoned and half off, her tongue on Katherine's smooth breast, when the doorbell rang.

All movement stopped. They looked at each other, eyes wide. The doorbell rang again. Katherine began closing her blouse. "Will you go to the door while I straighten my clothes? It's the furniture."

Marlena, her pulse still pounding, opened the door to a man with a clipboard in his hand. "Guess we're at the right place," he said, motioning two other men to open the huge van parked backward at the curb. As they began unloading, Katherine walked to the door, her clothing in place and buttoned.

"I'll take the list," she said, reaching for the clipboard. They stood aside as the men walked some things through the door and wheeled other things on a hand truck. In less than forty-five minutes they were finished. Katherine, who had checked off each piece as it came through the door, had a check ready.

As they closed the door behind them, Katherine said, "That was a hell of a time to be interrupted."

Marlena looked at her watch. "We still have time for a sandwich at the club. That OK with you?"

Nodding, Katherine asked, "Would it be OK with you if that's all we had, just a sandwich, but no upstairs? I really want to get started here. I'll make it up to you tonight."

Angela brought tea to their table. "I already ordered your sandwiches when I saw you pull up. They'll be ready in a minute." She was facing the swinging doors to the kitchen, and she started to say something else when the doors opened and Katherine saw Goliath, hands on hips, staring their way. Angela turned and almost ran to the kitchen doors, squeezing past her huge lover, who turned and followed.

There were several couples at adjoining tables, and Katherine heard low laughter as the swinging doors gradually stopped moving. "Told you," Marlena said, laughing.

"Would anyone in their right mind challenge that woman? I think Angela is perfectly safe." Katherine was laughing, too. They ate sandwiches, drank their tea, and went directly to Marlena's car.

"Katherine, if you want one more thing moved, I'm going to collapse." Marlena, hands on her hips, had just finished pushing the long, glass display case into another spot, where it was too jammed to put anything in it. "We've moved every damn piece ten times. You've got to make up your mind."

"I told you I wasn't a patient soul, but you're the one with no patience. We've only been at this . . ." Katherine looked at her watch. "My God, it's almost eight o'clock! What happened to the time?" She looked at a disheveled Marlena, who was leaning against the much-moved display case. "Come on, baby, let's go home."

They walked together up the stairs. Katherine, key ready, was about to unlock the door when she gasped. "The glass is broken!"

Marlena moved Katherine aside and stooped to

peer at the door. "Yes," she said calmly, "it certainly is." She turned to Katherine. "Stay calm, I'll call Tim." They waited on the landing for not more than six minutes until a police car pulled to the curb. Two uniformed men, one of whom Katherine recognized, walked up the stairs.

"I think it's our friend again," Marlena said. "I don't think she got into the house, but I'll feel better if you go in with us."

They searched the apartment, looked down the elevator shaft, and tried to open the door that led downstairs. "That's locked from the other side," Marlena told them. "No way to get through there." Tim and Marlena had a quiet private conversation, leaving Katherine and the other officer in the living room. After the men had closed the door behind them, Marlena embraced Katherine.

"This is going to stop, Katherine. I haven't done anything up until now, hoping that woman would go away, but it doesn't look like she will. Tonight was the last straw. I don't want you to worry anymore."

Katherine, who looked haunted, said, "I'm afraid, Marlena, because she's so unpredictable. She's going to ruin everything."

"I don't think so," Marlena said.

Chapter 15

Archie called before they left the house next morning. "You're famous!" she told Katherine excitedly. "Your picture was on the front page of our local paper. It's the one I took of you on the dock when we caught so many fish last summer. They took away the dock and the string of fish and just printed your face."

"Why was I in the paper?" Katherine interrupted. "Was it because of the book?"

"No, those two pictures you sent me, the ones with the man in it, the ones Bill Tangy asked for.

Well, he wanted the pictures because he figured the man had something to do with all the medical stuff floating in the river, and he was right! They identified the man and found where he was dumping, thanks to you. He's in jail now." Out of breath, Archie paused long enough for Katherine to ask a question.

"What medical stuff?"

"You haven't heard?" Archie was incredulous.

"No, I haven't heard anything. Why don't you tell me?"

Katherine winked at Marlena, who was finishing the last bite of a scrambled egg sandwich. Marlena looked at her watch and began gathering breakfast dishes.

"They started finding all kinds of medical things along the riverbank and even floating along the lakeshore. You mean you didn't read anything in the paper about it?" Archie couldn't believe it wasn't headline news in New Orleans, too.

"Archie, I haven't read a newspaper lately. I've been too busy. All I know is what your friend Bill told me, and that wasn't very much."

"Katherine, we've heard nothing else but! A little girl was stuck by a needle her little brother found in the river and they rushed her to the hospital, because of AIDS, you know."

"Oh, no! That's terrible," Katherine said. "What finally happened?"

"Bill told me they won't know for a couple of months. There's testing and stuff to do before they can tell whether or not. One good thing, Bill said the syringe and needle had been floating in the river for a while, and there was what he called the dilution factor to consider. He thinks there won't be any problem with AIDS, but hepatitis B and hepatitis C are possibilities, except a virus can't live in the sun, and maybe the syringe and needle sat for a while —"

Katherine interrupted. "Slow down, Archie. Bill told you all this? I guess he learned it at the hospital, right?"

"He told me all kinds of things I didn't know about infection, and he said the little girl wasn't the only one, either."

"Well, why was my picture in the paper?"

"Because it was you who took the picture of the man dumping those green bags in the rookery. You're our local celebrity. I told the reporter a little about you and about the book, and everybody's called me. Made me feel kind of important."

"Archie, do you have copies of the paper? I'd like to read about it. I suppose the papers here reported it, but I've not even seen a paper in weeks. You tell your friend Bill that I'm really glad I could help."

"Bad things happening?" Marlena asked when Katherine hung up.

"A man, the one I photographed without knowing I'd done it, was dumping medical waste in the rookery, and a little girl and some others have been stuck by needles that could have been used on AIDS patients. I think Archie said the man was in jail now."

"What a terrible thing! Do they know if anyone contracted AIDS?"

"Archie said there are tests still to be done. Can

you imagine someone doing something like that?" Katherine surveyed the table that Marlena had cleared. "Thank you for the cleanup job," she said. "If you weren't already working, I'd hire you."

"Working for you would be great; think of all the perks." Shutting her briefcase, Marlena leaned over for a good-bye kiss. "I won't be there for lunch, my love. I'm eating with the captain of the Naiad Carnival Krew today. Not only do I do the flowers for the ball, I'm also a line lieutenant."

"Is that more important than having lunch with me?"

"Nothing is more important than the time I spend with you, and you know it." Marlena reached for another kiss. "Would you be interested in taking a break around three o'clock? I should be finished by then."

"You're having a three-hour lunch? What does this captain look like, anyway?"

"Ah," Marlena said, lifting her eyebrows, "she's something to see. But you don't have to be jealous; there'll be at least fifteen other women."

"An orgy, my dear? Is that what you do at lunch?"

"That's what you and I do at lunch, why be different?" Marlena pulled Katherine into her arms, hugging tightly. "If I don't go," she whispered, "I can't get back."

"Then go, but I want you walking through the door no later than three, understand?" Katherine leaned back, looking at the smile on Marlena's face. "If you can manage to get away earlier than three, I might think of something nice for you, something you don't expect. Now, go!"

Katherine waited until she saw Marlena's car pull out of the driveway before she gathered her papers and purse and headed for Royal Street in the French Quarter. There was no street parking, of course, so she parked in the garage of a department store which fronted Canal. Walking two blocks down, she turned into a jewelry store. Twenty minutes later, she checked her car out of the garage and drove back to Canal Street.

At a quarter to three, Katherine heard a key in the back door. She picked up a small, wrapped package and stood so that Marlena would see her the instant the door opened. Marlena, rushing, almost knocked Katherine to the floor. They collided, arms clinging for support.

Instead of untangling, they embraced. "I have something for you, my darling," Katherine whispered in Marlena's ear.

"Is it what you promised this morning? If it is, I'm ready."

"No, silly, come sit on the couch."

"I'm early, you see, so what nice thing do I get?"

"This," Katherine said. "This is your surprise, and also a nice thing."

Marlena looked at what was obviously a ring box. She frowned. "What is it?" she asked, looking at Katherine.

"Open and see," Katherine said.

Marlena tore away the ribbon and wrapping, slowly opened the box, and drew in a sharp breath. She turned to Katherine. "This is just like yours," she said in a rush.

"Yes," Katherine said, taking the box from Marlena's hands. "It's exactly like mine." She lifted

Marlena's left hand, took the diamond band from the box, and slid it on Marlena's third finger. "If you ever decide we can't be together, just take off the ring."

Marlena was very near tears. She held up her hand, and the ring glittered in the overhead light. "This is the sweetest, the most wonderful thing anyone in the world has ever given me. I'll never take it off, never!"

"I hoped you'd say that."

Marlena began to cry. Katherine held her in a tight embrace until the sobs became sniffles. "Here," Katherine said, "wipe your nose."

Marlena took great shuddering breaths, trying to talk. "All my life I've been independent, Katherine. I enjoyed my friends and lovers, but I've always held a little back so that I couldn't be hurt." The sobs returned full force; Marlena was choking on the words she wanted to say.

"Hush, darling, you don't have to say another thing, I understand." Katherine pulled a wad of tissue from the box and wiped Marlena's tears. "Please stop crying. I want to hug you, but you're getting me all wet."

Marlena's sniffles turned to laughter. She held up her hand again, admiring the look of the ring on her finger. "Good thing diamonds don't dissolve or I'd have to go buy another, wouldn't I?"

Katherine also held up her hand. "See, we're twins."

"We're more than twins, Katherine," Marlena said seriously, her voice low. "I don't have words to tell you how much I love you, and I always get all choked up and emotional anyway, so I'll . . ."

Gently, Katherine's fingers touched Marlena's lips. "Hush, my darling." Katherine looked at the twin bands. "I thought we'd say tender things, sort of a ceremony, when I gave you the ring, but we don't need affirmations or promises or pledges, do we?" Now tears were brimming in Katherine's brown eyes. She dabbed at her face with the soggy tissues in her hand. "What we need is another box of tissue."

They ate at the club. "Now that the shop is finished, we have to find a name for it. We do have to call it something, don't we?" Katherine asked.

"What about all the supplies you're going to sell. Will they be delivered before we go?" Marlena had used her left hand exclusively throughout the meal, eating, drinking, and gesturing. Katherine was amused but pleased. "We leave for Alexandria on Monday, remember?" Marlena had taken on the job of official tour guide for their trip around the state.

Katherine remembered very well that they were to leave on Monday. "I know," she said. "I haven't forgotten. I have everything scheduled for delivery the week we get home, and that's because I don't feel safe with a store full of goodies and us gone for a month. Didn't we make this decision together?"

"Yes, I just wanted confirmation, my dear." Marlena was on her last sip of tea. She looked at Katherine, her question unspoken, but Katherine heard it anyway.

"Yes, we have time to go upstairs. In fact, I want to very much." Katherine reached across the table, her left hand claiming Marlena's left hand. They looked down at the two clasped hands, identical rings on each third finger, and they smiled into each other's eyes.

"Honeymoon?" Marlena mouthed.

Katherine nodded. "Honeymoon," she said.

Marlena was groaning. Katherine's fingers and tongue, working slowly in the moisture between Marlena's legs, had aroused Marlena to the point of desperation. "Please," she was saying, as she pulled Katherine's head tighter against her. "Please," she begged, leaving open whether she meant *please continue as you are* or *please give me more, I'm about to come*.

Katherine, guided by experience, chose to respond to the latter. Her lips surrounded Marlena's clitoris, her tongue circling the tiny organ, and her fingers pushed aside the swollen lips of Marlena's vulva, entering to fill the dark space with movement, then retreating, then entering and retreating again and again.

"Was that enough?" Katherine asked later, her mouth against Marlena's ear, the fingers of her hand still resting deep within Marlena's engorged flesh.

"No, but I need to rest a minute." Marlena's heart was still pounding, her breathing harsh. "Why don't you kneel over my face while I rest."

"Are you sure? I don't want you to have a heart attack on our honeymoon." Katherine moved to straddle Marlena's face, resting on her knees, her hands on the headboard. She felt Marlena's fingers exploring and then finding what they sought.

Katherine gasped as she felt the touch of Marlena's soft tongue. "Oh, God, that's wonderful!" Katherine breathed, trying to keep her hips still. "It feels different this way." She felt moisture running down her inner thighs. "I can't do this," she choked suddenly, unexpectedly, "I can't hold still!" And on that shrill note, Katherine felt her orgasm begin.

"It's like wave action," Katherine was saying, "like my insides were retreating, sucking everything back into a tiny place between my legs, then exploding upward and inward with such pleasure, I almost can't bear it." She giggled, "Then why do you suppose I want you to make love to me so often?"

"I suppose because it does feel so good. When I'm at work, I think of you, and I imagine myself making you come. How you moan and groan, and how hot I get when you ask me for more." Marlena stretched, her movement causing their sheet to fall beside the bed. "Do you think that's a sign we should go?"

"Have you ever spent the night here?" Katherine was curious.

"A couple of times. Why? Do you want to stay?"

"I'd like to stay for supper, then go home afterward. I still have to get my wardrobe in order for the trip."

"That means we'll have the rest of the afternoon to do some more honeymooning?" Marlena reached for Katherine without waiting for an answer.

"I'd like something cool to drink. Then I want to bathe and maybe I'll think about it." Katherine sat up and smiled down at Marlena, who was reaching for her again. Reaching with her left hand, Katherine noticed.

"I just figured out something," Katherine said. "I know why we spend so much time here. It's because you don't really enjoy being with me in the apartment. I thought you'd gotten past that, but I see you haven't."

"No," Marlena sighed, "I haven't. Then there's the noise we hear. I still don't know what to think about that, do you?"

"Well, we have almost a whole month away from the apartment and the noise. Let's spend some time thinking about both those things."

"I want you to take a look at the condo I told you about. That's still an option, you know." Marlena yawned and reached for the bedside phone. "Have to let staff know this room won't be available until after supper. Then I'll have something to drink sent up."

Chapter 16

"Hello," Katherine said.

"This is Bill Tangy, may I speak with Miss Duncan?"

"This is Katherine, Bill. Yesterday Archie called to tell me a little about the person dumping medical waste in the swamp. I'm certainly glad you caught him."

"That's why I called. Since your pictures put us on to what was happening and helped us identify the man, I thought you'd like to hear the entire story. Do you have time? If not, I can call back later."

"Yes, I'm very interested."

"OK. In the first place, we tried to identify the man from your picture. Folks at the hospital acknowledged they'd hired an outside person to haul their waste to a medical dump site upstate, and that's what they thought he was doing. They were paying to have it hauled and paying the dump fee, too. It amounted to a pretty fair sum."

"But he wasn't doing that at all, was he?"

"No'm, he wasn't. Well, within a day of having your photo of him in the paper, we had dozens of calls from people who recognized him. The name they gave us was the same as what the hospital told us, so we were able to get our hands on him without too much trouble." Bill paused, and Katherine heard voices in the background. "We picked him up, but he denied everything. Wasn't until we showed him the entire photo, that he confessed.

"There're not too many people who know about that rookery. To protect the birds, we don't talk about it, and it made us plenty mad at what he'd done. There were a couple of truckloads of stuff floating in the river, and more had drifted down to the lake. We've had volunteers scratching around to locate what we can so nobody else will get stuck or hurt. Least we hope not."

"What about the little girl? Will she be OK?"

"We all hope so. The water was fast flowing, so most of the stuff got diluted, too diluted to be of much harm except for bacteria from the stick itself. At the hospital they scrubbed her arm with plenty of soap and water and gave her a tetanus shot, too. They think a bacterial infection on her skin would be the worst she could get."

"I think that kind of infection can be treated with antibiotics, can't it?" Katherine was trying to remember her first aid.

"Yes'm, all those others who were in contact are getting the same treatment. See, viruses can't live in the sun, so the doctors told me, and if things didn't get washed in the river or the lake, the sun probably killed whatever didn't go into the water." Bill cleared his throat and continued. "At the hospital they tested right away for HIV. They'll test again after an incubation period and then do more testing at three months and six months. They're going to be very, very careful."

"Tell me about the man. What will happen to him?"

"He'll be prosecuted for dumping medical waste in an area not approved for it. There are also some minor things we can charge him with. The girl's family is suing him, and I think the city and state will do that, too. They probably won't get any money out of him, but they're sure to get a judgment. He's been in jail for doing other things. I think we ought to throw away the keys this time."

"I suppose he doesn't see the harm he could have done. He probably wouldn't have cared, whatever happened."Katherine was shaking her head in disgust.

"No'm, he wouldn't care. Fact is, he doesn't care even now. He thinks he's been railroaded, and he wants revenge for what we're doing to him. Especially he talks about getting even with you because your picture was what nailed him."

"Oh, dear. I'm glad he's in jail."

"We think he'll stay there for a while because he

can't make bail. Well, you take care ma'am, and we all want to thank you for the help you gave us. We woulda been up the creek without your pictures. We're really grateful."

"You're welcome. Give Archie my love when you see her."

"Bill said the man doesn't care about the harm he could have done to a lot of people," Katherine told Marlena as she packed that night. She noticed that Marlena kept looking at her hand, as if she had never worn a ring before.

"A lot of people are like that, Katherine. They just don't care about anything or anybody. I've known a few."

"Oh, come on! Who did you know?"

"My ex, Eva, that's one. She was selfish to the point of criminal activity, and I didn't realize it until our joint account shrank to nothing. You see, I'd put money in, and she'd take it out. Boy, was I stupid!"

"Not stupid, trusting."

"She either hocked or stole everything we had that was of any value in order to buy drugs for her new girlfriend. I had to catch them in the act."

"How awful that must have been for you."

"It was more a waste than awful. I lost eight good years." Marlena shrugged. "That's the way it is," she added. "Good she didn't touch any of Aunt Helen's things. Guess she knew we'd prosecute."

"I'll give you eight good years to make up for

those lost ones. How's that?" Katherine was trying to fold things so they wouldn't be crushed beyond recognition in her suitcase.

"You're going to give me eight years? I thought we were going to be together forever — at least that's what you promised. I'll bet you're the kind who'll say anything to get a little sex."

"We are going to be together forever. Now get off the bed so I can spread these things."

"We have all day tomorrow to pack, you know, so why are you doing it now? I, for one, am going to wait until the last minute."

"You're hoping your fairy godmother will do it for you, aren't you? Well I have news."

"But you'll give me a hand, won't you? Look at all that moving and hauling I did for you. Doesn't one good turn deserve another?"

"The next time you have furniture to move, call me. I'll supervise whoever does the actual moving. I'm good at that, as you know." Katherine refolded a nightgown so it would fit into a space where a toothpick couldn't be crammed.

"Why are you taking gowns, my dear? I've never seen you sleep in one." Marlena's eyes widened. "I guess that means it's over."

"You can always rip it off. I thought you liked to undress me." Katherine surveyed the suitcase and the clothing on the bed. She turned to look through the bedroom door at the living room couch. With her left hand, she began unbuttoning her blouse.

Marlena grinned. "Is this an invitation?" she asked.

"Take it any way you like. I'm going to be naked on that couch in about two minutes. You can do what you wish."

"My God, woman, are you never satisfied?" Marlena began pulling off her clothing, and by the time they reached the couch, they were both naked.

"I have a plan," Marlena announced as she spread syrup on her waffle. "I think you'll approve."

"Maybe, maybe not," Katherine answered, sipping coffee.

"You're worried about Pam; I can tell. You think she may get into your place while we're gone. OK, I think so, too, and I've thought of a way to take care of things while we're off in the boondocks." Marlena thought New Orleans was the only civilized city in Louisiana, and that just barely.

"I'm waiting," Katherine said, watching Marlena methodically cut a bite-size bit of waffle.

"I'm going to ask Angela and Tiny to stay in your place while we're not here. They occasionally house-sit for club members, and I know they'll do it for you if I ask."

"That monster of a woman is called 'Tiny'? I would never have guessed." Katherine couldn't help laughing as she remembered the few times she'd seen the club's cook.

"That's not her real name. Only the accountant knows what that is, but at one time or another we've seen her four sisters, and they're bigger than Tiny." Marlena gestured with her arms stretched their widest. "The oldest one is bigger than a dump truck."

"I have to think for a minute," Katherine said, buttering toast. She took a bite. "OK, I've thought about it. It's a good idea."

"We'll go this morning and ask." Marlena ate more waffle, making sure her left hand was visible most of the time.

"What, or how much, will we have to tell her? I don't like the thought of my problem with Pam becoming part of the local lore." Katherine was very pleased that Marlena liked her ring. *Our wedding ring*, Katherine thought.

"Dynamite couldn't pry a secret out of Tiny. Because of the nature of the club, we had to have someone who could keep her mouth closed, and Tiny knows everything that goes on; she knows everybody. We worried about Angela at first, but as silly as she is, she can be trusted. We've found that out over the seven years she's been with Tiny."

Katherine buttered more toast. "I'll take your word for it," she said.

"If they're going to do this, we haven't given them much time. Come on, let's go to the club."

Tiny listened as Marlena explained. Angela heard some of it, but she was waiting tables and was in the kitchen only part of the time. Tiny kept working as Marlena talked, and Katherine watched in amazement as Tiny filled breakfast orders as she listened.

"We'd start tonight?" Tiny reached for plates and began dividing scrambled eggs. When the piles were even, she arranged bacon, grits, and toast. Placing the plates on a table for Angela to collect, she added a sprig of parsley to each. "I think that'll be OK," she said, cracking more eggs over a huge frying pan.

"Here's my key." Marlena unclipped her apartment key from her key ring, and placed it on the table. "Use the driveway to park your car; anything you find to eat in the fridge is yours. There'll be room in the closet, and empty drawers for other things." Marlena was trying to remember everything.

Katherine was thinking. Then she said, "I won't get much mail, but will you collect it for me on the coffee table?" At Tiny's nod, Katherine continued, "The answering machine will take care of messages, and I might call you at night to hear what I have, if that's OK. Maybe you'll open letters if I think they're important or if they need an immediate reply."

"Sure," Tiny answered, her smile revealing even, white teeth. "Angela and I like adventures, and this sounds like one."

As they were leaving, Katherine asked, "I thought we were going to be home tonight and leave in the morning. Wasn't that what we decided?"

"I know, but Tiny and Angela are off on Monday. This way they have a whole day to settle in. You and I, my dear, will stay in Baton Rouge tonight. We will wine and dine at the finest." Marlena waited for Katherine to nod. "Good," she said, "I knew you'd like that idea."

"A thought just occurred to me. You haven't packed yet, and I'll bet you're going to want a lot of help, aren't you? I knew you had an ulterior motive."

"It's a wife's duty to help with packing." Marlena turned her attention from the road, and looked at

Katherine's astonished expression. They had not talked about who was to be called what in their relationship. Marlena didn't think Katherine was even aware of the butch-femme dichotomy.

Katherine was looking down at her clasped hands. "Am I your wife?" she asked softly. Marlena's declaration surprised Katherine. When she put the ring on Marlena's finger, to Katherine it had been a wedding band. But Marlena had never mentioned marriage, and Katherine thought Marlena meant it only as a gesture of friendship when she had bought the band Katherine now wore. But looking at Marlena, Katherine saw the gentle smile, the love it expressed, and knew what the rings signified for both of them.

"Yes, my darling," Marlena answered, "we can be whatever we like to each other — wife, husband, whatever. But when there are clothes to pack, you are the wife."

"Is that what the contract says?"

"It does the way I read it."

"I packed so fast I'm sure everything you own is wrinkled to death. First, we're going to hang things, and then I'll fold and repack. I can't have you looking like a stepchild."

"Why do you think people will be looking at me? I believe you will be the center of attention, my dear, you and your book."

"Well, let's hope so. It's a very expensive book; not everybody will be able to afford it. I think it's worth what the university is charging, though."

Turning back to her folding, Katherine said, "This is a very nice suite. It's so luxurious it feels sinful."

"Do you realize this is our first night in a real hotel? I think we're supposed to be sinful, except that we're not cheating on anybody. This is probably the start of our honeymoon; what we've done before was practice."

Katherine stopped folding. She walked over to Marlena, sat on the chair's armrest, and kissed the top of Marlena's head. Marlena pulled Katherine into her lap. "We have almost a whole month to be together," she said. "It's the start of our lifetime with each other."

Katherine snuggled in Marlena's arms. "Why am I thinking of your Aunt Helen?" she asked. "We haven't heard the noises for a while. I don't know what brought it on."

"I do," Marlena answered. "I know it's because we're starting our life together, and Aunt Helen and Marlena didn't get to have the life they dreamed about. That'll always be a sad memory; they were so much in love." Marlena paused. "I love you that much, too," she said, tightening her arms around Katherine.

They stayed like that for a while, not moving, warm bodies close, and two hearts beating in a gentle rhythm.

Later that night, after lovemaking that felt different for both of them, they whispered in the silent room. "I wanted you so very much," Marlena said, "but loving you wasn't the same. I felt a difference. Did you?"

Katherine smiled; Marlena heard it in her voice. "You were your usual frantic self, my darling, and I responded with as much excitement as always but, yes, I felt something different, too. I believe we were truly making love. No, we were giving love."

"Come," Marlena said, "put your head on my shoulder. I want to sleep with you in my arms."

"Yes," Katherine said, "oh, yes."

The man sitting at the bar had been drinking beer for hours. His long, dank hair, close-set eyes, and filthy jeans and shirt kept the stools on both sides of him empty. He did a lot of muttering and slobbering, peering suspiciously at the bills and change on the bar in front of him as the bartender deducted for his drinks. After his family had put in for bail, he had asked for money for his pocket. Grudgingly, they had given him thirty dollars, most of which he'd already spent for beer.

"I'm going to get that bitch," he was heard to say.

Chapter 17

Marlena's sports car whizzed along the highway to Alexandria, in central Louisiana. The miles seemed to fly by as they talked and laughed. Katherine remarked delightedly, "We're getting to know each other."

"Yes." Marlena smirked, glancing sideways at Katherine. "Yes, we're beginning to *know* each other quite well."

"Don't be ugly. You know what I meant."

"OK, then here's something I don't know. How can Pam stay away from work so long? Doesn't she have a job in Mobile? How can she afford to hang around just to annoy you?"

"I'm not sure. She doesn't have any money to speak of, or a full-time job. She does have cousins in New Orleans who're probably letting her stay with them. I have no idea where she's getting money. Also, I have no idea why she's harassing me."

Deftly swinging the car around an eighteen-wheeler, Marlena returned to the proper lane. "She's just pissed off, I guess."

"I guess." Katherine watched the roadside greenery for a while. "I think she's never been the one to end a relationship, if that's what we had. My leaving was a real blow to her pride." More greenery flew by. "Marlena, I really think she wants to hurt me . . . hurt me physically, I mean."

"Not to be mean spirited, but I almost hope she tries to break in. Won't she be surprised?"

Katherine snorted. "I don't think *surprise* is the word. I, for one, wouldn't want to tangle with Tiny. She's so huge!"

"She's intimidating, yes, but I think underneath those muscles she's probably a pussycat. We've never known anyone to cross her about anything, not that anyone in their right mind would do that deliberately."

"They make such a picture. Tiny and Angela, I mean."

"The picture I would have paid to see is Tiny protecting Angela from a motorcycle gang."

"When was this?" Katherine asked.

"The story I heard, Angela was waiting bar when these guys started giving her trouble. Tiny was minding the bar for one of her sisters, and she saw they'd reduced Angela to tears, so she walked around the bar, picked up the gang leader, and threw him out the plateglass window. I was told she didn't say one word; she just grabbed the next guy and he lit on the parking lot gravel next to the first."

Katherine was doubled over with laughter. Marlena started laughing so hard she could hardly finish the story. "By this time, the motorcycles were roaring out of the lot, almost on top of each other. Tiny stood in the doorway until they were all gone, and then she walked back behind the bar and started pouring beer, not even winded."

"And Angela?"

"Nobody knows how it came about, but the next night they walked in together, Tiny towering protectively over Angela, and Angela all smiles, her eyes hardly leaving Tiny for an instant. They've been together since then."

"Know what I think? Tiny pretends to be jealous because it pleases Angela. Even an idiot wouldn't make a pass at Angela, and Tiny knows it."

"You're right. None of the idiots I know would even think about it. That's how Angela can get away with flirting; nobody ever takes her up on it." Marlena swerved off the highway. "How does Ralph's Diner sound to you. They have good food and lots of it."

"You've been here before?"

"I used to have a girlfriend in Marksville so I drove up once in a while. I'd stop here for a meal."

Ralph's Diner wasn't like a diner at all. It was a flat, one-story building that had probably been a warehouse. The decor was flaking paint, the tables cigarette burned, the menu spotted with remains of meals served in antiquity. The food, however, was home cooked and delicious.

Marlena waited for Katherine's comment, which came after only a few bites. "This is the best I've eaten; even Archie's cooking can't compare."

"Told you," Marlena said, pleased.

After eating until they couldn't, they sat drinking tea and talking. "I don't like to keep thinking about Pam, but there has to be something we can do if she keeps hounding me. I don't suppose the police can help until she's maimed me in some way."

"We'll see about that. Tim is gay. He'll have a pocketful of tricks. We'll have a talk as soon as we get back." Marlena was trying to be reassuring.

"What if Pam learns about the store? She could just drop by any time, and I'll be alone for the most part. I hate to think she could trap me in the back room."

"Whoa, that's not going to happen. You're only a few blocks from me; we'll have some sort of alarm that'll alert me or the people in my place. We can get to you in a couple of minutes. Honestly, love, I won't let her hurt you."

Katherine smiled across the table at Marlena. "I know," she said.

There was a message at the desk from Dr. Beale. Katherine read it and turned to Marlena. "Think we can stop a day in Monroe and one in Shreveport? I have no idea where these places are, but they want a signing, too. She says we can also loop down to Lake Charles for one day and then go on to Lafayette as scheduled. We certainly have the time, except that we'd planned to drift along between signings. This means we'll have to hop to it."

Marlena said, "I'll need a map. I'm not too familiar with the roads up there."

The desk clerk had a map. They went to their room and Marlena spread the map on the bed. "Doesn't look too bad," she said, "but you'd better call Dr. Beale to get correct dates and times. We could get awfully screwed up. We won't try to get reservations; there are usually plenty of vacant rooms at roadside motels."

Katherine was emptying suitcases. "I'd better call the store here in town to confirm the time I'm supposed to be there tomorrow. It's on the schedule, but you never know."

The bookstore owner was delighted to hear from Katherine. They were very excited about the book, she said, and were looking forward to tomorrow.

"Well, we can have a leisurely breakfast, maybe look around town for a while, then be there half an hour before you go on stage." Marlena folded the map. "Do you realize I haven't hugged you since morning? I haven't even touched your hand."

Katherine arched her eyebrows. "Oh," she said. "I hadn't noticed."

"Listen, smartie, we're on our honeymoon, and I intend to continue the orgy we started last night, whether you noticed or not. Put down those damn clothes and come here." She held out her arms.

* * * * *

Katherine was amazed at the number of people waiting for her signature. They were all holding a copy of *Big Cypress*. Katherine smiled, signed, had a pleasant word for each, and then looked up at the next person. She had thought it would be a book women were more likely to buy, but there were men in line, too. The bookstore owner was wearing a smile larger than life; she was probably selling more than she expected.

When Katherine's two hours were finished, she and Marlena couldn't leave the store because of several customers who wanted to talk with the photographer. They wanted technical information about the photographic process. Katherine, remembering when she was learning, tried to be helpful. Marlena stayed in the background, beaming as if Katherine were her discovery.

In the car, Katherine said, "I still have a kind of buzz. I had no idea what it felt like to have people want your autograph. And thank you, darling, for waiting. You are my loving patient soul." She reached to pat Marlena's thigh, leaving her hand there as they sped toward the motel.

Marlena pulled into the motel lot, parking in front of their door. "If we're going to Monroe, we can leave now, stay the night there, and you won't be so rushed in the morning. How's that sound?"

"OK by me. Now I wished I hadn't unpacked everything we own. I'll just have to repack, I guess."

"I'll help," Marlena offered.

They checked out and were on the road to Monroe within an hour. It wasn't a terribly long drive, and they registered at a very nice motel around dark. When the door closed behind them, Marlena said, "I know coming here is an interruption in the lazy schedule we'd planned, but I'm enjoying every minute." She held out her arms in invitation. "Let's enjoy the next few minutes, too."

Later they sent out for food. They were sound asleep by midnight. As Katherine drifted, she replayed the day. The signing had been fun. The ride through Louisiana's rural area had been pleasant, but Marlena's loving caress, the feel of her mouth and tongue, were remembered more clearly than anything else. Katherine slept with her body pressed against Marlena's warm flesh.

The book signing in Monroe was much like Alexandria. They left right after the signing, eating on the way, and registering in Shreveport late that afternoon. Katherine called New Orleans and listened while Dr. Beale talked at length about the baby herons and Katherine's photographs of the heron family. She reminded Katherine that everyone thought another book, this one of Katherine's experience with the chicks, would be a fine thing for children. Would Katherine think seriously about doing it? Dr. Beale asked.

When Dr. Beale hung up, Katherine sighed with relief. Turning to Marlena, who was fiddling with the TV, she said, "I am not an author, I'm a photographer. I did write most of the text for the photographs, but that wasn't like writing a book. I don't think I have a book in me."

Not finding a program worth watching, Marlena

punched the OFF button. "How do you know?" she asked. "Wouldn't you have to write something in order to find out?"

"I like my little shop. I know about cameras and photographic equipment, and I'm damn good at what I do. There's no time for writing books on my agenda. I don't think I want to find out whether I could or not."

"Well, you have time to think about it, but call the bookstore now so we'll be on time tomorrow."

When Katherine finished that call, she called Tiny. "No news is good news," she said to Marlena, who was stepping out of the shower. "There hasn't been any trouble, although they did hear someone on the steps during the night. Tiny said they're enjoying the apartment, and is it ever going to be for rent?"

"Ah," Marlena said, "this leads us back to the question of the entire house. Have you thought about the condo? Would you like to go see it? Do you realize that we need more space than the apartment has for the two of us? Do you have any idea what you'd like to do?"

"Questions, questions." Katherine began taking off her clothes. "What I'm going to do is shower. We can talk later."

Marlena watched Katherine, admiring her firm breasts, her slim waist, and her fiery-red pubic hair. "I love you, Katherine Duncan. I love you very much," she said simply.

"Enough to shower again . . . with me?" Katherine asked.

* * * * *

Signing in Shreveport was much the same as Alexandria and Monroe, and Katherine was pleased. "I like signing because it makes me feel important, sought after. I also have decided about the condo. I'd like to see it."

"Soon as we get home," Marlena said. She was already convinced that moving was the best thing for them to do. The apartment and the house were filled with memories. Pam was not an important consideration; she could be taken care of when they returned to New Orleans. They'd start their new life with a clean slate.

Because the schedule allowed, they stayed the night in Shreveport, leaving early in the morning for Lake Charles. Katherine had a day before she had to appear at the bookstore, so they stopped often along the way, mostly at roadside stands displaying homemade, handmade crafts.

"What will we do with all this?" Katherine moaned, looking at the bags and boxes in the tiny backseat.

"How about Tiny and Angela? The women at my stores like to be remembered; we'll have something for each of them."

"Speaking of Tiny, she said they heard noises the last two nights. From what she said, I couldn't tell if it was Pam at the door or someone else on the landing. The thought occurred to me that it may have been that ass from across the lake, although I don't want to believe he could be sneaking around. I didn't question Tiny too closely. We'll wait until we're home."

"Maybe it was Aunt Helen downstairs again. We certainly haven't heard her much lately."

"Let me tell you what I think, OK?" Katherine took a deep breath. "First, you know I don't believe in spirits or ghosts, but we both heard something... or somebody." Katherine watched Marlena nod in agreement. "We were both saddened by Aunt Helen's lost love, and we wanted to think they were finally together and happy even if they were both dead." Marlena was nodding. "Well, we were so impressed by that thought that we both heard sounds, only we didn't compare to see that we were hearing the same sounds, just that we heard sounds."

Marlena shrugged. Katherine continued, "Isn't it possible that you heard one thing and I heard another? Both of us were listening with our hearts, not our ears. We wanted them to be together, happy and making love, like we were, so we thought we heard what we wanted to hear." Katherine waited for Marlena to respond.

"You're probably right; I just never thought about it that way." Marlena watched Katherine smile, thinking that Katherine had heard the noises before she knew anything about Aunt Helen and Marlena. She hadn't even known their names. *What is the explanation for that?* Marlena wondered.

"So, if the house does become a museum, which it is already, there won't be any strange noises to hear." This was Katherine's last word on the subject.

Of course there won't be any more noises, Marlena thought, *because Aunt Helen was letting me know things were finally OK with her. She'd have no reason to tell strangers*. And, this was Marlena's final thought on the same subject.

Chapter 18

The book signing in Lake Charles was a success. They left immediately for Lafayette, which was only a few hours away.

Lafayette was a charming Southern town; Katherine liked everything about it. "There's a race-track," Marlena said. "How do you feel about horse racing?"

"I don't feel much of anything. I've never been." Katherine shrugged; she wasn't a gambler. While combing through her unruly curls, she watched

Marlena in the mirror. "Do you want to go?" she asked.

"There are several well-known restaurants in town. We could have some Cajun food and then go throw money away at the track." Marlena enjoyed the casinos and the track, but she wasn't really into gambling either.

"I do like horses, so that may be fun. What does one wear?"

"Slacks are OK. I'm glad we had the cleaners do a job on our clothes or I'd have to go bare-assed."

"I'll get ready. Would it be OK, do you think, if I called Tiny at the club? I've had a strange feeling all day, something to do with New Orleans, I think." Katherine didn't say that the feelings were more than strange. She had been anxious and on edge. There was nothing she could point to that caused her apprehension. She just had an uneasy feeling that something was wrong.

"Sure, call her," Marlena said from the shower.

"Well, we did have some excitement." Tiny laughed. "It was your girlfriend. She decided to break in. Somehow she unlocked the kitchen door, and we were there waiting." Tiny sounded gleeful. "Your girlfriend is a real case, let me tell you! I don't know why you were scared of her."

If Katherine had been standing, her knees would have given way. "Dear God, I hope you're all right."

"Sure, we're OK. No problem. Call us tonight and we'll fill you in, but you don't have to worry about Miss Pam any more."

Katherine hurried into the bathroom and yanked

aside the shower curtain. "Pam tried to break in last night," she said in a rush, her eyes wide.

"Who did what?" Marlena asked, squinting, her head a tower of suds.

Later, calmer, Katherine reported what Tiny had said. "I don't have to worry any more about Pam, and Tiny doesn't know why I was worried in the first place."

Marlena snorted. "If I were ten feet tall with muscles like a weight lifter I wouldn't worry either. Tiny forgets that her size insulates her from trouble. We mortals of ordinary stature don't have that convenience."

"Horses are beautiful," Katherine decided, watching them parade before the race. "I wonder if there's a book of horse photos around?"

"Only about a million." Marlena was busy tearing up losing tickets. "Drat," she said. "This is why I don't gamble."

"Did you lose, darling? I won." Katherine held up her money. "You see, I bet on the color of the horse, not all that gibberish you worked over in that book." Katherine came away with sixty dollars; Marlena lost over a hundred.

Later, hearing the full story of Pam and her abortive attempt to do whatever it was she had in mind, both Katherine and Marlena laughed until tears ran.

"I didn't turn on a light," Tiny reported, "but I stood in the dark and waited. It took her a while until she had the door open, and when she stepped in, I grabbed her. You should have heard her squeal!"

Angela took over. "My baby lifted that bitch right off her feet and crammed her head against the ceiling, wham! She didn't know what had her, and she was so scared she peed in her pants. She didn't even kick or wave her arms or nothing. In fact, she couldn't even talk."

"That's when I told her what would happen if she ever came within a mile of Katherine or the apartment. I told her to get her ass back to Mobile, and if Katherine even thought the bitch was coming near, that I'd see to it both legs, both arms, and most of her ribs would be a long time healing." Tiny paused for breath. "Then I walked her to the landing and leaned her over the railing. She found her voice then."

"Yeah," Angela interrupted, "she was begging for her life, and all's I could do was laugh. We booted her down the stairs and went back to bed. I don't think you have to worry any more, Katherine, especially since Tiny told her she had four sisters, all bigger than she is."

"Having Tiny and Angela in the apartment was a wonderful idea," Katherine said. "I feel sure Pam won't bother me again, but," she considered, "I almost feel sorry for her. It must be terrible to have such a violent comedown."

"Don't fret, baby, I'm just glad you don't have to worry about her anymore."

"Do I have to worry about the man from across the lake? He might have been doing more than just talking. Trash like that probably thinks the world is against them, and now he has the name of a person who really did him harm."

"You didn't do him harm. It wasn't your idea for him to pollute the area; he did all that on his own." Marlena once had misgivings about Pam, and the trouble Pam could have caused, but a lowlife, asshole man was something else. Marlena did worry about what he might feel compelled to do in order to punish Katherine. *I can certainly have Tim patrol the area, maybe even hire a private agency at night*, she thought. None of her feelings were evident to Katherine, however, and the book signing went very well. Their trip back to New Orleans across the Atchafalaya Swamp, which stretched for miles in all directions, was a revelation to Katherine.

"I thought I was photographing a swamp," she told Marlena, "but this place defies imagination. I'm glad my book covered a smaller area, because I don't think I would have enjoyed spending days and nights crouched in a tiny canoe in this place."

"Your swamp was more interesting, especially the baby herons. I think you should consider using your photos of them in another book."

Marlena looked at Katherine, who was gnawing a thumbnail, a thoughtful expression on her face. "I guess I could think about it, couldn't I?" Katherine asked.

Marlena had told Tiny to wait until Monday to move out of the apartment so that she and Angela wouldn't be rushed. "We, my love, are going to stay in the French Quarter, in elegance and luxury, and take time to look at the condo. Then we'll wine and dine at fabulous places, stroll the streets, et cetera."

"Sounds fine to me," Katherine said, "but could we spare a minute or two to check on the shop? And we can't forget the book signing on Canal Street Friday."

"All of those things are on the list, my dear."

"Then let's go loll in luxury for a while, shall we?" Katherine made a mental note to call Dr. Beale, to find out if the date and time of her book signing had been changed.

On the way to the condo, they stopped at Katherine's shop. Everything was as they had left it. Katherine made another mental note to call the supply house and arrange delivery next week. "I'm going to have fun arranging things," she told Marlena. "I've always liked to do that."

"I'll help if you don't make me haul that damn display case around the room again. My back still aches thinking about it."

"If your back aches, it's not from the display case, my dear."

"Whatever can you mean?" Marlena asked, grinning.

Katherine was impressed as they drove under the condo's porte cochere. "This is really elegant," she breathed as the doorman rushed to assist them. "Are you sure we're in the right place?"

"I think it's going to be the right place for us. If you like it, that is." The manager escorted them to the elevator and through a very ornate door at the center of the fifth-floor hall. "This is the one you called about, Miss Weathers, and it's ready for occupancy, of course."

Katherine's eyes kept getting wider as he led them through room after room. "I'll leave you and Miss Duncan now. Please, take all the time you want." He bowed himself out.

"What do you think?" Marlena asked. "Too big, not big enough, what?"

"Marlena, I've never lived in a place like this. What do we need with a formal dining room, a dinette, and a table in the kitchen? This is almost as big as your museum."

"You are an author now; you must keep up appearances. It wouldn't hurt for me to step up a rung on the social ladder either, and this is a place for doing that. Do you think you could be happy here?"

"Happy, yes, but I can't afford half. I probably can't afford the water bill. It's beautiful, but way out of my reach, and I don't even know how much it is."

"We do have to buy it, of course, but it won't be a strain on my finances. I'm a wealthy dyke, my dear. Anyway, who said anything about half?"

Katherine shook her head. "I'm not wealthy, Marlena, and I can't —"

"Sh, don't say another word. Let's wait until we're back at the hotel, OK?"

Katherine was silent as they sped back to the Quarter. She was almost in tears.

Shutting their door, Marlena faced Katherine, who was now sobbing. She led Katherine to a chair, then knelt, looking up at the misery on Katherine's face. "Will you just listen to me, please?" At Katherine's nod, she continued, "I know why you're crying," she said softly. "You're too proud to accept anything else from me, aren't you? Giving you the shop was a mistake, but it made me happy, and because I'm selfish, I did it."

Katherine's sobs increased. Marlena reached to touch the tears. "All my life I've wanted someone to love with my whole heart. I loved Eva, but not the way I love you. I can't begin to tell you how I feel. I don't have the words. But I do have money, and I guess I try to tell you by using money instead of words. It's the only way I know."

Now Marlena began crying. She stood, her body shaking with great, tearing sobs. "Here," she said after a moment, "take your ring. You're free again." She dropped the ring into Katherine's lap, and turned to the door.

"If you walk out that door, who's going to move the display case for me?"

Marlena stopped, her back still turned, shoulders stiff. "I told you my back already hurt from last time," she said, her voice shaking.

"Come here, let's see if I can do something about that."

Marlena turned. Katherine was standing, her arms reaching.

"Were we fighting?" Katherine asked later.

Marlena lifted her head from Katherine's breast.

"I don't know what to call what we were doing. Having a good cry, I think." She took Katherine's nipple into her mouth again.

"Know what?" Katherine whispered.

"Ummm," Marlena breathed, her tongue moving in lazy circles around Katherine's breast.

"Remember when I knelt over your face? Remember what you did?" Katherine's voice was quiet. Marlena had to strain, but she heard.

"Want to do that again?"

"Please."

"Let me slide up a bit; now kneel, and I'll give you what you want."

"I like it when you say things like that," Katherine said as she knelt. She felt the tip of Marlena's tongue touch delicately, then move slowly through folds of moist flesh. "Go in me," she pleaded, and Marlena's tongue stabbed upward. To Katherine, it felt both hard and soft at the same time. As before, Katherine cried out, her body arching. She clung to the headboard, trying to remain upright until the spasms stopped.

"Did I give you what you wanted?"

"Yes. I don't think I'll ever get enough, though."

"That's OK by me." Marlena sat up, and, looking down at Katherine, asked, "Can we talk now? I've waited until you were sated, like now, and too weak to argue." Marlena watched Katherine smile. "I need to know if it's all right with you if I have the most money. I can't help being rich, and I haven't done much of anything to earn it, but I want you in every way, so please let's just use what we need. The condo, too."

"If that will make you happy, it will make me

happy. Now, let's call down for food. If we can afford it, that is."

Katherine was surprised at the lateness of the hour. "Where did the time go?"

"Why? Are you going somewhere?"

"Is it too late to call Tiny, do you think? I'm having another psychic spell." Marlena handed her the phone.

"Yes, we've had some trouble, but it's over now," Tiny reported. "Some piece of white trash tried to break in. I'm telling you, Katherine, you ought to get another kind of door. Angela has been sweeping up glass for hours. A good solid wooden door would be better than all that glass."

"Please, Tiny, just tell me what happened." Katherine motioned for Marlena, and they shared the handset as Tiny talked.

"This guy was falling-down drunk. He bashed in the glass, and when he couldn't open the lock, he kicked open the door. Broke it away from the hinges, and it fell smack on the floor. I was waiting this time, too, so I grabbed him and threw him off the balcony. Shoulda thrown harder, I guess, because he landed in the shrubs instead of on the concrete."

Katherine and Marlena stared at each other, mouths open.

"We called the police, and they hauled him away to the hospital. Far as I know, he's only got one or two bones unbroken, and when he heals he'll be in jail for a long time. I told your friend, Tim, who the man was, and why he was trying to get in the apartment. There won't be any trouble about it, except you need a new door."

Marlena broke in, "Tiny, do you and Angela want the apartment? When it gets a new door, that is."

"Sure we do. It's close to work, plenty big enough, and it's got such nice stuff. Sure, we'd like to have it."

"It's yours! I think the house will need a caretaker, so you won't owe rent if you agree to keep your eyes open around the place. The downstairs is going to be a museum, and you'll probably get a caretaker's salary, too. Listen, we'll work out the details later, OK?"

"Sure, that's fine with us." Marlena and Katherine both heard Angela's squeal of delight as they hung up.

Katherine threw her arms around Marlena. Showering kisses, she said, "This has been one fine day, my love. We've solved all our problems, haven't we?"

"Not quite," Marlena said, trying to catch Katherine's mouth. "Now we have to select stuff for the condo, and I hate looking at furniture."

"Leave everything to me," Katherine said. She touched Marlena's lips. They kissed softly, a chaste kiss that lasted and lasted.

"Guess what?" Katherine breathed when their lips parted for a moment.

"Ah," Marlena said, taking Katherine's hand. "I know what."

A few of the publications of
THE NAIAD PRESS, INC.
P.O. Box 10543 Tallahassee, Florida 32302
Phone (850) 539-5965
Toll-Free Order Number: 1-800-533-1973
Web Site: WWW.NAIADPRESS.COM
Mail orders welcome. Please include 15% postage.
Write or call for our free catalog which also features an incredible selection of lesbian videos.

FALLEN FROM GRACE by Pat Welch. 256 pp. 6th Helen Black mystery.	ISBN 1-56280-209-7	$11.95
THE NAKED EYE by Catherine Ennis. 208 pp. Her lover in the camera's eye . . .	ISBN 1-56280-210-0	11.95
OVER THE LINE by Tracey Richardson. 176 pp. 2nd Stevie Houston mystery.	ISBN 1-56280-202-X	11.95
JULIA'S SONG by Ann O'Leary. 208 pp. Strangely disturbing . . . strangely exciting.	ISBN 1-56280-197-X	11.95
LOVE IN THE BALANCE by Marianne K. Martin. 256 pp. Weighing the costs of love . . .	ISBN 1-56280-199-6	11.95
PIECE OF MY HEART by Julia Watts. 208 pp. All the stuff that dreams are made of —	ISBN 1-56280-206-2	11.95
MAKING UP FOR LOST TIME by Karin Kallmaker. 240 pp. Nobody does it better . . .	ISBN 1-56280-196-1	11.95
GOLD FEVER by Lyn Denison. 224 pp. By author of *Dream Lover.*	ISBN 1-56280-201-1	11.95
WHEN THE DEAD SPEAK by Therese Szymanski. 224 pp. 2nd Brett Higgins mystery.	ISBN 1-56280-198-8	11.95
FOURTH DOWN by Kate Calloway. 240 pp. 4th Cassidy James mystery.	ISBN 1-56280-205-4	11.95
A MOMENT'S INDISCRETION by Peggy J. Herring. 176 pp. There's a fine line between love and lust . . .	ISBN 1-56280-194-5	11.95
CITY LIGHTS/COUNTRY CANDLES by Penny Hayes. 208 pp. About the women she has known . . .	ISBN 1-56280-195-3	11.95
POSSESSIONS by Kaye Davis. 240 pp. 2nd Maris Middleton mystery.	ISBN 1-56280-192-9	11.95
A QUESTION OF LOVE by Saxon Bennett. 208 pp. Every woman is granted one great love.	ISBN 1-56280-205-4	11.95

RHYTHM TIDE by Frankie J. Jones. 160 pp. . . . to desire passionately and be passionately desired. ISBN 1-56280-189-9 11.95

PENN VALLEY PHOENIX by Janet McClellan. 208 pp. 2nd Tru North Mystery. ISBN 1-56280-200-3 11.95

BY RESERVATION ONLY by Jackie Calhoun. 240 pp. A chance for true happiness. ISBN 1-56280-191-0 11.95

OLD BLACK MAGIC by Jaye Maiman. 272 pp. 9th Robin Miller mystery. ISBN 1-56280-175-9 11.95

LEGACY OF LOVE by Marianne K. Martin. 240 pp. Women will do anything for her . . . ISBN 1-56280-184-8 11.95

LETTING GO by Ann O'Leary. 160 pp. Laura, at 39, in love with 23-year-old Kate. ISBN 1-56280-183-X 11.95

LADY BE GOOD edited by Barbara Grier and Christine Cassidy. 288 pp. Erotic stories by Naiad Press authors. ISBN 1-56280-180-5 14.95

CHAIN LETTER by Claire McNab. 288 pp. 9th Carol Ashton mystery. ISBN 1-56280-181-3 11.95

NIGHT VISION by Laura Adams. 256 pp. Erotic fantasy romance by "famous" author. ISBN 1-56280-182-1 11.95

SEA TO SHINING SEA by Lisa Shapiro. 256 pp. Unable to resist the raging passion . . . ISBN 1-56280-177-5 11.95

THIRD DEGREE by Kate Calloway. 224 pp. 3rd Cassidy James mystery. ISBN 1-56280-185-6 11.95

WHEN THE DANCING STOPS by Therese Szymanski. 272 pp. 1st Brett Higgins mystery. ISBN 1-56280-186-4 11.95

PHASES OF THE MOON by Julia Watts. 192 pp. . . . . hungry for everything life has to offer. ISBN 1-56280-176-7 11.95

BABY IT'S COLD by Jaye Maiman. 256 pp. 5th Robin Miller mystery. ISBN 1-56280-156-2 10.95

CLASS REUNION by Linda Hill. 176 pp. The girl from her past . . . ISBN 1-56280-178-3 11.95

DREAM LOVER by Lyn Denison. 224 pp. A soft, sensuous, romantic fantasy. ISBN 1-56280-173-1 11.95

FORTY LOVE by Diana Simmonds. 288 pp. Joyous, heart-warming romance. ISBN 1-56280-171-6 11.95

IN THE MOOD by Robbi Sommers. 160 pp. The queen of erotic tension! ISBN 1-56280-172-4 11.95

SWIMMING CAT COVE by Lauren Douglas. 192 pp. 2nd Allison O'Neil Mystery. ISBN 1-56280-168-6 11.95

THE LOVING LESBIAN by Claire McNab and Sharon Gedan. 240 pp. Explore the experiences that make lesbian love unique. ISBN 1-56280-169-4 14.95

COURTED by Celia Cohen. 160 pp. Sparkling romantic encounter.	ISBN 1-56280-166-X	11.95
SEASONS OF THE HEART by Jackie Calhoun. 240 pp. Romance through the years.	ISBN 1-56280-167-8	11.95
K. C. BOMBER by Janet McClellan. 208 pp. 1st Tru North mystery.	ISBN 1-56280-157-0	11.95
LAST RITES by Tracey Richardson. 192 pp. 1st Stevie Houston mystery.	ISBN 1-56280-164-3	11.95
EMBRACE IN MOTION by Karin Kallmaker. 256 pp. A whirlwind love affair.	ISBN 1-56280-165-1	11.95
HOT CHECK by Peggy J. Herring. 192 pp. Will workaholic Alice fall for guitarist Ricky?	ISBN 1-56280-163-5	11.95
OLD TIES by Saxon Bennett. 176 pp. Can Cleo surrender to a passionate new love?	ISBN 1-56280-159-7	11.95
LOVE ON THE LINE by Laura DeHart Young. 176 pp. Will Stef win Kay's heart?	ISBN 1-56280-162-7	11.95
DEVIL'S LEG CROSSING by Kaye Davis. 192 pp. 1st Maris Middleton mystery.	ISBN 1-56280-158-9	11.95
COSTA BRAVA by Marta Balletbo Coll. 144 pp. Read the book, see the movie!	ISBN 1-56280-153-8	11.95
MEETING MAGDALENE & OTHER STORIES by Marilyn Freeman. 144 pp. Read the book, see the movie!	ISBN 1-56280-170-8	11.95
SECOND FIDDLE by Kate 208 pp. 2nd P.I. Cassidy James mystery.	ISBN 1-56280-169-6	11.95
LAUREL by Isabel Miller. 128 pp. By the author of the beloved *Patience and Sarah.*	ISBN 1-56280-146-5	10.95
LOVE OR MONEY by Jackie Calhoun. 240 pp. The romance of real life.	ISBN 1-56280-147-3	10.95
SMOKE AND MIRRORS by Pat Welch. 224 pp. 5th Helen Black Mystery.	ISBN 1-56280-143-0	10.95
DANCING IN THE DARK edited by Barbara Grier & Christine Cassidy. 272 pp. Erotic love stories by Naiad Press authors.	ISBN 1-56280-144-9	14.95
TIME AND TIME AGAIN by Catherine Ennis. 176 pp. Passionate love affair.	ISBN 1-56280-145-7	10.95
PAXTON COURT by Diane Salvatore. 256 pp. Erotic and wickedly funny contemporary tale about the business of learning to live together.	ISBN 1-56280-114-7	10.95
INNER CIRCLE by Claire McNab. 208 pp. 8th Carol Ashton Mystery.	ISBN 1-56280-135-X	11.95

LESBIAN SEX: AN ORAL HISTORY by Susan Johnson. 240 pp. Need we say more? ISBN 1-56280-142-2 14.95

WILD THINGS by Karin Kallmaker. 240 pp. By the undisputed mistress of lesbian romance. ISBN 1-56280-139-2 11.95

THE GIRL NEXT DOOR by Mindy Kaplan. 208 pp. Just what you d expect. ISBN 1-56280-140-6 11.95

NOW AND THEN by Penny Hayes. 240 pp. Romance on the westward journey. ISBN 1-56280-121-X 11.95

HEART ON FIRE by Diana Simmonds. 176 pp. The romantic and erotic rival of *Curious Wine.* ISBN 1-56280-152-X 11.95

DEATH AT LAVENDER BAY by Lauren Wright Douglas. 208 pp. 1st Allison O'Neil Mystery. ISBN 1-56280-085-X 11.95

YES I SAID YES I WILL by Judith McDaniel. 272 pp. Hot romance by famous author. ISBN 1-56280-138-4 11.95

FORBIDDEN FIRES by Margaret C. Anderson. Edited by Mathilda Hills. 176 pp. Famous author's "unpublished" Lesbian romance. ISBN 1-56280-123-6 21.95

SIDE TRACKS by Teresa Stores. 160 pp. Gender-bending Lesbians on the road. ISBN 1-56280-122-8 10.95

HOODED MURDER by Annette Van Dyke. 176 pp. 1st Jessie Batelle Mystery. ISBN 1-56280-134-1 10.95

WILDWOOD FLOWERS by Julia Watts. 208 pp. Hilarious and heart-warming tale of true love. ISBN 1-56280-127-9 10.95

NEVER SAY NEVER by Linda Hill. 224 pp. Rule #1: Never get involved with . . . ISBN 1-56280-126-0 11.95

THE SEARCH by Melanie McAllester. 240 pp. Exciting top cop Tenny Mendoza case. ISBN 1-56280-150-3 10.95

THE WISH LIST by Saxon Bennett. 192 pp. Romance through the years. ISBN 1-56280-125-2 10.95

FIRST IMPRESSIONS by Kate 208 pp. 1st P.I. Cassidy James mystery. ISBN 1-56280-133-3 10.95

OUT OF THE NIGHT by Kris Bruyer. 192 pp. Spine-tingling thriller. ISBN 1-56280-120-1 10.95

NORTHERN BLUE by Tracey Richardson. 224 pp. Police recruits Miki & Miranda — passion in the line of fire. ISBN 1-56280-118-X 10.95

LOVE'S HARVEST by Peggy J. Herring. 176 pp. by the author of *Once More With Feeling.* ISBN 1-56280-117-1 10.95

THE COLOR OF WINTER by Lisa Shapiro. 208 pp. Romantic love beyond your wildest dreams. ISBN 1-56280-116-3 10.95

FAMILY SECRETS by Laura DeHart Young. 208 pp. Enthralling romance and suspense. ISBN 1-56280-119-8 10.95

INLAND PASSAGE by Jane Rule. 288 pp. Tales exploring conventional & unconventional relationships. ISBN 0-930044-56-8 10.95

DOUBLE BLUFF by Claire McNab. 208 pp. 7th Carol Ashton Mystery. ISBN 1-56280-096-5 10.95

BAR GIRLS by Lauran Hoffman. 176 pp. See the movie, read the book! ISBN 1-56280-115-5 10.95

THE FIRST TIME EVER edited by Barbara Grier & Christine Cassidy. 272 pp. Love stories by Naiad Press authors. ISBN 1-56280-086-8 14.95

MISS PETTIBONE AND MISS McGRAW by Brenda Weathers. 208 pp. A charming ghostly love story. ISBN 1-56280-151-1 10.95

CHANGES by Jackie Calhoun. 208 pp. Involved romance and relationships. ISBN 1-56280-083-3 10.95

FAIR PLAY by Rose Beecham. 256 pp. An Amanda Valentine Mystery. ISBN 1-56280-081-7 10.95

PAYBACK by Celia Cohen. 176 pp. A gripping thriller of romance, revenge and betrayal. ISBN 1-56280-084-1 10.95

THE BEACH AFFAIR by Barbara Johnson. 224 pp. Sizzling summer romance/mystery/intrigue. ISBN 1-56280-090-6 10.95

GETTING THERE by Robbi Sommers. 192 pp. Nobody does it like Robbi! ISBN 1-56280-099-X 10.95

FINAL CUT by Lisa Haddock. 208 pp. 2nd Carmen Ramirez Mystery. ISBN 1-56280-088-4 10.95

FLASHPOINT by Katherine V. Forrest. 256 pp. A Lesbian blockbuster! ISBN 1-56280-079-5 10.95

CLAIRE OF THE MOON by Nicole Conn. Audio Book — Read by Marianne Hyatt. ISBN 1-56280-113-9 16.95

FOR LOVE AND FOR LIFE: INTIMATE PORTRAITS OF LESBIAN COUPLES by Susan Johnson. 224 pp. ISBN 1-56280-091-4 14.95

DEVOTION by Mindy Kaplan. 192 pp. See the movie — read the book! ISBN 1-56280-093-0 10.95

SOMEONE TO WATCH by Jaye Maiman. 272 pp. 4th Robin Miller Mystery. ISBN 1-56280-095-7 10.95

GREENER THAN GRASS by Jennifer Fulton. 208 pp. A young woman — a stranger in her bed. ISBN 1-56280-092-2 10.95

TRAVELS WITH DIANA HUNTER by Regine Sands. Erotic lesbian romp. Audio Book (2 cassettes) ISBN 1-56280-107-4 16.95

CABIN FEVER by Carol Schmidt. 256 pp. Sizzling suspense and passion. ISBN 1-56280-089-1 10.95

THERE WILL BE NO GOODBYES by Laura DeHart Young. 192 pp. Romantic love, strength, and friendship. ISBN 1-56280-103-1 10.95

FAULTLINE by Sheila Ortiz Taylor. 144 pp. Joyous comic lesbian novel. ISBN 1-56280-108-2 9.95

OPEN HOUSE by Pat Welch. 176 pp. 4th Helen Black Mystery. ISBN 1-56280-102-3 10.95

ONCE MORE WITH FEELING by Peggy J. Herring. 240 pp. Lighthearted, loving romantic adventure. ISBN 1-56280-089-2 11.95

FOREVER by Evelyn Kennedy. 224 pp. Passionate romance — love overcoming all obstacles. ISBN 1-56280-094-9 10.95

WHISPERS by Kris Bruyer. 176 pp. Romantic ghost story. ISBN 1-56280-082-5 10.95

NIGHT SONGS by Penny Mickelbury. 224 pp. 2nd Gianna Maglione Mystery. ISBN 1-56280-097-3 10.95

GETTING TO THE POINT by Teresa Stores. 256 pp. Classic southern Lesbian novel. ISBN 1-56280-100-7 10.95

PAINTED MOON by Karin Kallmaker. 224 pp. Delicious Kallmaker romance. ISBN 1-56280-075-2 11.95

THE MYSTERIOUS NAIAD edited by Katherine V. Forrest & Barbara Grier. 320 pp. Love stories by Naiad Press authors. ISBN 1-56280-074-4 14.95

DAUGHTERS OF A CORAL DAWN by Katherine V. Forrest. 240 pp. Tenth Anniversay Edition. ISBN 1-56280-104-X 11.95

BODY GUARD by Claire McNab. 208 pp. 6th Carol Ashton Mystery. ISBN 1-56280-073-6 11.95

CACTUS LOVE by Lee Lynch. 192 pp. Stories by the beloved storyteller. ISBN 1-56280-071-X 9.95

SECOND GUESS by Rose Beecham. 216 pp. An Amanda Valentine Mystery. ISBN 1-56280-069-8 9.95

A RAGE OF MAIDENS by Lauren Wright Douglas. 240 pp. 6th Caitlin Reece Mystery. ISBN 1-56280-068-X 10.95

TRIPLE EXPOSURE by Jackie Calhoun. 224 pp. Romantic drama involving many characters. ISBN 1-56280-067-1 10.95

PERSONAL ADS by Robbi Sommers. 176 pp. Sizzling short stories. ISBN 1-56280-059-0 11.95

CROSSWORDS by Penny Sumner. 256 pp. 2nd Victoria Cross Mystery. ISBN 1-56280-064-7 9.95

SWEET CHERRY WINE by Carol Schmidt. 224 pp. A novel of suspense. ISBN 1-56280-063-9 9.95

CERTAIN SMILES by Dorothy Tell. 160 pp. Erotic short stories. ISBN 1-56280-066-3 9.95

EDITED OUT by Lisa Haddock. 224 pp. 1st Carmen Ramirez Mystery. ISBN 1-56280-077-9 9.95

WEDNESDAY NIGHTS by Camarin Grae. 288 pp. Sexy adventure. ISBN 1-56280-060-4 10.95

SMOKEY O by Celia Cohen. 176 pp. Relationships on the playing field. ISBN 1-56280-057-4 9.95

KATHLEEN O'DONALD by Penny Hayes. 256 pp. Rose and Kathleen find each other and employment in 1909 NYC. ISBN 1-56280-070-1 9.95

STAYING HOME by Elisabeth Nonas. 256 pp. Molly and Alix want a baby . . . or do they? ISBN 1-56280-076-0 10.95

TRUE LOVE by Jennifer Fulton. 240 pp. Six lesbians searching for love in all the "right" places. ISBN 1-56280-035-3 11.95

KEEPING SECRETS by Penny Mickelbury. 208 pp. 1st Gianna Maglione Mystery. ISBN 1-56280-052-3 9.95

THE ROMANTIC NAIAD edited by Katherine V. Forrest & Barbara Grier. 336 pp. Love stories by Naiad Press authors. ISBN 1-56280-054-X 14.95

UNDER MY SKIN by Jaye Maiman. 336 pp. 3rd Robin Miller Mystery. ISBN 1-56280-049-3. 11.95

CAR POOL by Karin Kallmaker. 272pp. Lesbians on wheels and then some! ISBN 1-56280-048-5 10.95

NOT TELLING MOTHER: STORIES FROM A LIFE by Diane Salvatore. 176 pp. Her 3rd novel. ISBN 1-56280-044-2 9.95

GOBLIN MARKET by Lauren Wright Douglas. 240pp. 5th Caitlin Reece Mystery. ISBN 1-56280-047-7 10.95

FRIENDS AND LOVERS by Jackie Calhoun. 224 pp. Mid-western Lesbian lives and loves. ISBN 1-56280-041-8 11.95

BEHIND CLOSED DOORS by Robbi Sommers. 192 pp. Hot, erotic short stories. ISBN 1-56280-039-6 11.95

CLAIRE OF THE MOON by Nicole Conn. 192 pp. See the movie — read the book! ISBN 1-56280-038-8 11.95

SILENT HEART by Claire McNab. 192 pp. Exotic Lesbian romance. ISBN 1-56280-036-1 11.95

THE SPY IN QUESTION by Amanda Kyle Williams. 256 pp. A Madison McGuire Mystery. ISBN 1-56280-037-X 9.95

SAVING GRACE by Jennifer Fulton. 240 pp. Adventure and romantic entanglement. ISBN 1-56280-051-5 10.95

CURIOUS WINE by Katherine V. Forrest. 176 pp. Tenth Anniversary Edition. The most popular contemporary Lesbian love story. ISBN 1-56280-053-1 11.95

Audio Book (2 cassettes) ISBN 1-56280-105-8 16.95

CHAUTAUQUA by Catherine Ennis. 192 pp. Exciting, romantic adventure. ISBN 1-56280-032-9 9.95

A PROPER BURIAL by Pat Welch. 192 pp. 3rd Helen Black Mystery. ISBN 1-56280-033-7 9.95

SILVERLAKE HEAT: A Novel of Suspense by Carol Schmidt. 240 pp. Rhonda is as hot as Laney's dreams. ISBN 1-56280-031-0 9.95

LOVE, ZENA BETH by Diane Salvatore. 224 pp. The most talked about lesbian novel of the nineties! ISBN 1-56280-030-2 10.95

A DOORYARD FULL OF FLOWERS by Isabel Miller. 160 pp. Stories incl. 2 sequels to *Patience and Sarah.* ISBN 1-56280-029-9 9.95

MURDER BY TRADITION by Katherine V. Forrest. 288 pp. 4th Kate Delafield Mystery. ISBN 1-56280-002-7 11.95

THE EROTIC NAIAD edited by Katherine V. Forrest & Barbara Grier. 224 pp. Love stories by Naiad Press authors. ISBN 1-56280-026-4 14.95

DEAD CERTAIN by Claire McNab. 224 pp. 5th Carol Ashton Mystery. ISBN 1-56280-027-2 9.95

CRAZY FOR LOVING by Jaye Maiman. 320 pp. 2nd Robin Miller Mystery. ISBN 1-56280-025-6 11.95

UNCERTAIN COMPANIONS by Robbi Sommers. 204 pp. Steamy, erotic novel. ISBN 1-56280-017-5 11.95

A TIGER'S HEART by Lauren W. Douglas. 240 pp. 4th Caitlin Reece Mystery. ISBN 1-56280-018-3 9.95

PAPERBACK ROMANCE by Karin Kallmaker. 256 pp. A delicious romance. ISBN 1-56280-019-1 10.95

THE LAVENDER HOUSE MURDER by Nikki Baker. 224 pp. 2nd Virginia Kelly Mystery. ISBN 1-56280-012-4 9.95

PASSION BAY by Jennifer Fulton. 224 pp. Passionate romance, virgin beaches, tropical skies. ISBN 1-56280-028-0 10.95

STICKS AND STONES by Jackie Calhoun. 208 pp. Contemporary lesbian lives and loves. ISBN 1-56280-020-5 9.95
Audio Book (2 cassettes) ISBN 1-56280-106-6 16.95

UNDER THE SOUTHERN CROSS by Claire McNab. 192 pp. Romantic nights Down Under. ISBN 1-56280-011-6 11.95

GRASSY FLATS by Penny Hayes. 256 pp. Lesbian romance in the '30s. ISBN 1-56280-010-8 9.95

THE END OF APRIL by Penny Sumner. 240 pp. 1st Victoria Cross Mystery. ISBN 1-56280-007-8 8.95

KISS AND TELL by Robbi Sommers. 192 pp. Scorching stories by the author of *Pleasures.* ISBN 1-56280-005-1 11.95

STILL WATERS by Pat Welch. 208 pp. 2nd Helen Black Mystery. ISBN 0-941483-97-5 9.95

TO LOVE AGAIN by Evelyn Kennedy. 208 pp. Wildly romantic love story. ISBN 0-941483-85-1 11.95

IN THE GAME by Nikki Baker. 192 pp. 1st Virginia Kelly Mystery. ISBN 1-56280-004-3 9.95

STRANDED by Camarin Grae. 320 pp. Entertaining, riveting adventure. ISBN 0-941483-99-1 9.95

THE DAUGHTERS OF ARTEMIS by Lauren Wright Douglas. 240 pp. 3rd Caitlin Reece Mystery. ISBN 0-941483-95-9 9.95

CLEARWATER by Catherine Ennis. 176 pp. Romantic secrets of a small Louisiana town. ISBN 0-941483-65-7 8.95

THE HALLELUJAH MURDERS by Dorothy Tell. 176 pp. 2nd Poppy Dillworth Mystery. ISBN 0-941483-88-6 8.95

SECOND CHANCE by Jackie Calhoun. 256 pp. Contemporary Lesbian lives and loves. ISBN 0-941483-93-2 9.95

BENEDICTION by Diane Salvatore. 272 pp. Striking, contemporary romantic novel. ISBN 0-941483-90-8 11.95

TOUCHWOOD by Karin Kallmaker. 240 pp. Loving, May/December romance. ISBN 0-941483-76-2 11.95

COP OUT by Claire McNab. 208 pp. 4th Carol Ashton Mystery. ISBN 0-941483-84-3 10.95

THE BEVERLY MALIBU by Katherine V. Forrest. 288 pp. 3rd Kate Delafield Mystery. ISBN 0-941483-48-7 11.95

THE PROVIDENCE FILE by Amanda Kyle Williams. 256 pp. A Madison McGuire Mystery. ISBN 0-941483-92-4 8.95

I LEFT MY HEART by Jaye Maiman. 320 pp. 1st Robin Miller Mystery. ISBN 0-941483-72-X 11.95

THE PRICE OF SALT by Patricia Highsmith (writing as Claire Morgan). 288 pp. Classic lesbian novel, first issued in 1952 . . . acknowledged by its author under her own, very famous, name. ISBN 1-56280-003-5 10.95

SIDE BY SIDE by Isabel Miller. 256 pp. From beloved author of *Patience and Sarah.* ISBN 0-941483-77-0 10.95

STAYING POWER: LONG TERM LESBIAN COUPLES by Susan E. Johnson. 352 pp. Joys of coupledom. ISBN 0-941-483-75-4 14.95

SLICK by Camarin Grae. 304 pp. Exotic, erotic adventure. ISBN 0-941483-74-6 9.95

NINTH LIFE by Lauren Wright Douglas. 256 pp. 2nd Caitlin Reece Mystery. ISBN 0-941483-50-9 9.95

PLAYERS by Robbi Sommers. 192 pp. Sizzling, erotic novel. ISBN 0-941483-73-8 9.95

MURDER AT RED ROOK RANCH by Dorothy Tell. 224 pp. 1st Poppy Dillworth Mystery. ISBN 0-941483-80-0 8.95

A ROOM FULL OF WOMEN by Elisabeth Nonas. 256 pp. Contemporary Lesbian lives. ISBN 0-941483-69-X 9.95

THEME FOR DIVERSE INSTRUMENTS by Jane Rule. 208 pp. Powerful romantic lesbian stories.	ISBN 0-941483-63-0	8.95
CLUB 12 by Amanda Kyle Williams. 288 pp. Espionage thriller featuring a lesbian agent!	ISBN 0-941483-64-9	9.95
DEATH DOWN UNDER by Claire McNab. 240 pp. 3rd Carol Ashton Mystery.	ISBN 0-941483-39-8	10.95
MONTANA FEATHERS by Penny Hayes. 256 pp. Vivian and Elizabeth find love in frontier Montana.	ISBN 0-941483-61-4	9.95
LIFESTYLES by Jackie Calhoun. 224 pp. Contemporary Lesbian lives and loves.	ISBN 0-941483-57-6	10.95
MURDER BY THE BOOK by Pat Welch. 256 pp. 1st Helen Black Mystery.	ISBN 0-941483-59-2	9.95
THERE'S SOMETHING I'VE BEEN MEANING TO TELL YOU Ed. by Loralee MacPike. 288 pp. Gay men and lesbians coming out to their children.	ISBN 0-941483-44-4	9.95
LIFTING BELLY by Gertrude Stein. Ed. by Rebecca Mark. 104 pp. Erotic poetry.	ISBN 0-941483-51-7	10.95
AFTER THE FIRE by Jane Rule. 256 pp. Warm, human novel by this incomparable author.	ISBN 0-941483-45-2	8.95
PLEASURES by Robbi Sommers. 204 pp. Unprecedented eroticism.	ISBN 0-941483-49-5	11.95
EDGEWISE by Camarin Grae. 372 pp. Spellbinding adventure.	ISBN 0-941483-19-3	9.95
FATAL REUNION by Claire McNab. 224 pp. 2nd Carol Ashton Mystery.	ISBN 0-941483-40-1	11.95
IN EVERY PORT by Karin Kallmaker. 228 pp. Jessica's sexy, adventuresome travels.	ISBN 0-941483-37-7	11.95
OF LOVE AND GLORY by Evelyn Kennedy. 192 pp. Exciting WWII romance.	ISBN 0-941483-32-0	10.95
CLICKING STONES by Nancy Tyler Glenn. 288 pp. Love transcending time.	ISBN 0-941483-31-2	9.95
SOUTH OF THE LINE by Catherine Ennis. 216 pp. Civil War adventure.	ISBN 0-941483-29-0	8.95
WOMAN PLUS WOMAN by Dolores Klaich. 300 pp. Supurb Lesbian overview.	ISBN 0-941483-28-2	9.95

These are just a few of the many Naiad Press titles — we are the oldest and largest lesbian/feminist publishing company in the world. We also offer an enormous selection of lesbian video products. Please request a complete catalog. We offer personal service; we encourage and welcome direct mail orders from individuals who have limited access to bookstores carrying our publications.